What You Need from the Night

What You Need from the Night

Laurent Petitmangin

TRANSLATED FROM THE FRENCH BY
Shaun Whiteside

Other Press
New York

Copyright © Laurent Petitmangin 2020
First published in French as *Ce qu'il faut de nuit* in 2020
by La Manufacture de Livres, Paris

English translation copyright © Shaun Whiteside 2023
First published in the English language in the United Kingdom by
Picador, an imprint of Macmillan Publishers International Limited.

Production editor: Yvonne E. Cárdenas
Typeset by Palimpsest Book Production Ltd, Falkirk, Stirlingshire, Scotland
This book was set in Apollo MT

1 3 5 7 9 10 8 6 4 2

Library of Congress Cataloging-in-Publication Data
Names: Petitmangin, Laurent, 1965- author. | Whiteside, Shaun, translator.
Title: What you need from the night / Laurent Petitmangin ;
translated from the French by Shaun Whiteside.
Other titles: Ce qu'il faut de nuit. English
Description: New York : Other Press, [2023] | First published in French
as Ce qu'il faut de nuit in 2020 by La Manufacture de Livres, Paris.
Identifiers: LCCN 2023000583 (print) | LCCN 2023000584 (ebook) |
ISBN 9781635423501 (paperback ; acid-free paper) | ISBN 9781635423518 (ebook)
Subjects: LCGFT: Novels.
Classification: LCC PQ2716.E897 C413 2023 (print) | LCC PQ2716.E897 (ebook) |
DDC 843/.92—dc23/eng/20230201
LC record available at https://lccn.loc.gov/2023000583
LC ebook record available at https://lccn.loc.gov/2023000584

What You Need from the Night

FUS CHARGES ACROSS the pitch. He goes in for a tackle. He likes tackling. He does it well, without throwing his opponent off course too much, but viciously enough to stop him for a moment. Sometimes the other guy fights back, but Fus is big, and when he's playing he looks mean. He's been called Fus since he was three. Fus is short for *Fussball*. Luxembourg-style. No one calls him anything else anymore. He's Fus to his teachers, to his mates, to me, his dad. I watch him playing every Sunday. Come rain or frost. Leaning on the barrier, apart from the others. The pitch is a long way from everything, framed by poplar trees, with the car park at the bottom of the hill. The little shack used for serving drink and snacks and storing equipment was repainted last year. The grass has been excellent for a few seasons although nobody knows why. And the air's always cool, even at the height of summer. No noise, just the motorway in the distance, a faint hum that keeps us in the world. A lovely place. You'd almost think it was a pitch for posh people. You'd have to go fifteen kilometers up to Luxembourg to find a better-kept pitch. I have my spot. Far away from the seats, far away from the little group of loyal fans. Also far away from the visiting team's supporters. A direct view of the only hoarding at the field, the kebab stand that does everything – pizza, tacos, the American (steak and chips in a half-baguette) – or the Stein (white pudding and chips, also in a half-baguette). Some people, like Mohammed, come and shake my hand, "Insh'Allah we'll destroy 'em – is Fus on form today?" and then go off again. I never get worked up, I never complain like the others do, I just wait for the match to be over.

This is my Sunday morning: I get up at seven, make coffee for Fus, give him a shout, he wakes up straight away without a word of complaint even if he went to bed late the previous evening. I wouldn't like to have to push it, to have to shake him, but it's never happened. I say through the door: "Fus, get up, time to get going," and he's in the kitchen a few minutes later. We don't usually speak. If we do, it's about the previous day's Metz game. We're in department 54, but locally we support Metz, not Nancy. That's just how it is. We always keep an eye on our car when we park it near the stadium. There are idiots everywhere, morons who get worked up at the sight of a "54" registration, and who are quite capable of giving your car a going over. If it's the day after a match I read him the report from the paper. We have our favorite players, the untouchables. The ones who will leave sooner or later. The club doesn't know how to keep them. They get lured away as soon as they start to shine. We're left with the rest, the sloggers, the ones we shout at twenty times a match, telling ourselves that they should get the hell out of here, we've had enough of their bullshit. All in all, if they get their jerseys wet, even when they've got two left feet, they can stay. We know what we're worth and we know how to make do.

When I watch Fus play I tell myself that there's no other life, no life apart from this one. There's this moment of people shouting, the sound of studs making contact with the grass and pulling away again, the shouts of his teammate, the one he doesn't get to quite on time, not playing deep enough, that rage they yell from the depths of their throats when scoring or conceding their first goal. A moment when there's nothing I need to be doing, one of the only moments I still have with Fus. A moment that I wouldn't lose for anything in the world, the moment I wait for more than anything else throughout the week. The one that gives me nothing but the fact of being there, that resolves nothing, nothing at all. When the game is over Fus doesn't come back straight away. I don't wait for him, and he doesn't show up until his brother and I have nearly finished lunch. "Hey, Fatboy, wash my kit?" "Oh sure, and why would I do that?" "You're my little brother, don't worry, I'll make it up to you." He picks up his plate, serves himself and goes and sits down in front of afternoon TV.

At five o'clock, when I can face it, I go up to the clubhouse. There are fewer and fewer people there since they stopped doing early evening drinks. It had gone nuts, the guys had stopped working and they just waited for the bottles to come out. There are four or five of us, rarely more than that. Not always the same ones. There's no need to unfold the big tables the way we did twenty years ago. Most of us don't work on Mondays. Pensioners, Lucienne – "la" Lucienne, we would say around here – who comes along as she did in her husband's day, with a cake that she cuts up nicely. Nobody says a word until she's cut eight lovely slices, all the same size. One or two of the guys have been unemployed since the Dark Ages. The topics are always the same, the village school that can't last when it's losing a class every three years, the shops getting boarded up one after the other, the elections. We haven't won for years. No one here voted for Macron. Nor for that other one either. That Sunday we all stayed at home. Even so, we were a bit relieved that she didn't go through. And I still wonder, though, if deep down some people mightn't rather she had.

We hand out the odd leaflet. I don't think it achieves that much, but there's one young guy who has a way with words. A guy who can sum up in a page the shit that our coal mines and our lives are drowning in. Jérémy. Not "le" Jérémy, just Jérémy plain and simple, because he's not from round here and he's forever taking the piss out of us for putting "le" or "la" in front of everyone's names. His parents came here fifteen years ago when the engine-casing factory was setting up its new production line. Forty jobs all at once. Unimaginable. If they haven't launched that line twenty times they've never launched it at all. The whole region, the prefect, the deputy, every class in the school turned up to wet themselves about it.

Even the priest who came to bless it several times on the quiet. The journalist from *Le Républicain* was forever turning up to go on about the conveyor belt, which she reckoned was a symbol, if you could believe that. "Lorraine is industrial and it will remain so." A pretty blonde doing her job as she was supposed to with suitably optimistic words. She took the photographs as well, and she varied the shots so that the Villerupt–Audun-le-Tiche page didn't look the same every day. That conveyor belt was a long time being launched, perhaps too long. The day they'd finally trained all the foremen and the operators, the day they'd finally found a way of dealing with the problem of the solvent – not a huge deal, just a leakage of a few centiliters a day that stopped them getting their accreditation – and they were back in the middle of a crisis, one with the banks this time, the one that would ultimately finish off the production line and everything that went with it. The factory could have been spewing out radioactive material and I don't think I'm lying when I say the village couldn't have cared less, they'd sooner have drunk water from the toilets than slowed down the launch of that production line. There wasn't much debate about it at the section, we weren't all that eco-aware at the time. Still aren't, in fact. Jérémy was part of what we used to call the "springtime class," a couple of dozen kids who turned up in March and April whose parents had just been hired, and who had taken a couple of catch-up classes by the start of the following school year.

Jérémy's twenty-three, a year younger than Fus. At first the two of them were mates. Fus liked him. He brought him to our house a few times, and he didn't bring a lot of people home. I think he felt a bit ashamed. Of his mother who could barely leave her bed. Maybe of me. Whenever Jérémy came it was a lovely day for my wife. If she had the strength she would get up and make waffles or beignets. She yelled at Fus a bit and said he should have told her, she'd have made the dough sooner, the day before, it would have been a lot better, but she ended up making those beignets of hers, crisp and sugar-glazed. There were enough of them for dinner with a big bowlful left over for the next day. Jérémy and Fus went on seeing each other till middle school. And then Fus's schoolwork started getting worse. He started bunking off. Not going to class. He had ready-made excuses. Hospital. His mother. His mother's illness. The few good days that we needed to take advantage of. His mother's final days. Mourning for his mother. Three terrible years, sixth grade–fifth grade–fourth grade, when he saw me completely powerless. Unable to believe it. Having lost all faith in a recovery that wouldn't come. Not even capable of giving up smoking. No longer capable of sitting down next to him, when he was crying on his bed, no longer capable of lying to him, telling him that *la moman* would be fine, that she might come back to us. Just about capable of feeding him and his brother. Just capable of rebuking myself for having children too late. We were both thirty-four when our Gillou was born.

By his final year in middle school Fus had stopped keeping up. He dropped the last of the friends he still had from the good times, when the teachers of the littler classes still liked him. The middle-school teachers were a lot less patient. They acted as if there was nothing going on. As if the boy wasn't spending his Sundays at Bon-Secours. At first he used to take his homework to the hospice, then he did the same as me, he just sat down by the bed, he looked at the bed, his mother in the bed, but most of all the bed, the covers, the way they were arranged. The little flaws in the weave from being boiled and bleached. For hours on end. It was hard to look at *la moman*, she had turned ugly. Forty-four. You'd have thought she was twenty, thirty years older. Sometimes the nurses made her up a bit but they couldn't hide the ocher tone that was slowly invading her exhausted face week after week, and particularly her arms sticking out from under the blanket, already at the end of life. Like me, he must sometimes have wanted just not to go to the hospice, just to have a normal Sunday, or else have wished for some kind of freak event to stop us setting off, but it never happened, we had nothing better to do, nothing more urgent, so we went to see *la moman* at the hospital. Sometimes we had to leave Gillou with the neighbors for the afternoon. On the stroke of eight, when they served dinner, we came out relieved to have left. Sometimes in the summer we were glad we'd opened the window. That we'd taken advantage of one of those hours when she was conscious, and listened with her to the noises coming from the courtyard. We lied to her, we told her she was looking better and that the consultant we'd bumped into in the corridor seemed pleased with her.

Still, I should have pushed him. I watched him slide back little by little. His marks weren't as good as before, but what did that matter? I used the little energy I still had to go on working, to go on keeping up appearances in front of my colleagues and the boss, to make sure I kept that lousy job. Taking care, exhausted as I was and sometimes a bit pissed, not to do anything stupid. Looking out for short circuits. Looking out for power drops. Overhead cables are a long way up. Get home safe and sound. Because I had to see to it that my two little weirdos got fed, making sure I didn't start drinking till they'd gone to bed. And then I'd let myself go. Not always. Often, though. That's how we made it through those three years. The hospice, the Longwy railway depot, sometimes the one at Montigny, the Aubange–Mont-Saint-Martin line, the Woippy marshalling yard, the house, the union branch and the new Bon-Secours. And then the nights away at Sarreguemines and Forbach, seeing to it that the neighbors could keep an eye on Gillou and Fus. Fus who had to prepare the food, ready meals, all he had to do was heat them up: "Be careful, don't forget the gas, don't set fire to the house on us. Don't go to bed too late, if you need to go and see Jacky, he knows you're on your own this evening." Fus was a grown-up from the age of thirteen. He had a man's responsibilities. A good lad, and the house was always spick and span when I came home the next day. He didn't once go and see Jacky. Not even when the hail shattered the kitchen window, hailstones big as your fist. Not even when Gillou couldn't sleep, he was frightened because he wanted his mother. Fus had always managed. He did what had to be done. He talked to Gillou, he woke him up the next day, made his breakfast. And still found time to clean up after himself. In other circumstances he would have been a model child, rewarded twenty times, a hundred times, a thousand times over. Here, with all the things that were going on, it had never occurred to me to say thank you. Just "Everything go OK, no mess-ups? We'll go to the hospice on Sunday." *La moman* knew how to look after Fus and Gillou. She went to all the school meetings and insisted that I take a day off and come along too. We were always the first to arrive, sat in the front row, wedged in behind the little primary-school desks. Listening attentively to the teacher's advice. *La moman* took notes that she read back to the kids in the evening. She had put Fus down for Latin, because the best ones did Latin, it helped you get a grasp of grammar, it was organization, like maths. Latin and German. They'd have plenty of time to do English in fourth grade. She was ambitious for both of them. "You'll be engineers with the railway service. There are decent jobs. Doctors too, but most importantly railway engineers." When her illness was discovered, she talked to me again about the children's future, but that was just at the start. I didn't believe in that cancer, and I don't think she did either. I'd heard the news without paying attention, and then she'd slipped quite quickly into suffering and never recovered from it. Over the last few weeks, when she knew it was over, she hadn't reviewed her life, she hadn't issued advice. She'd just looked at us for those small moments when she was conscious. Just observing us, not even smiling. She made me no promises. She left us. She had struggled with her cancer for three years, without ever saying that she was going to make it out the other side. *La moman* wasn't one for bragging. I'd once said to her: "You're going to do it for the kids." She replied, "I'm the one I'm doing it for." But I think she riled the doctors, she wasn't motivated enough, or at least not defiant enough. They waited for her to fight back, to say like the others that she was going to grab this cancer by the seat of its pants and send it packing. But she didn't say that. That was something for films, for other people. Like final instructions. Too much for her. It wasn't real life, it wasn't what her life was like in any case. And nobody at her funeral talked to me about her courage.

But three years of hospice, of chemo, three years of radiation. People had talked to me about me, about the children and what we were going to do now, hardly at all about her. It was as if they were a bit resentful of her resignation, of the poor image she gave of herself. The consultant had just shrugged his shoulders when I asked him how her last hours had been. "Like the days before, no more or less. You know, your wife never really rebelled against her illness. It's not something everyone can do. Incidentally, I'm not saying that it would have changed anything, no one can say that, in fact." That was his oration. Even the priest struggled. He didn't know us that well. Never went to mass, but *la moman* wanted some sort of service, or I imagine she did, we'd barely talked about it. I'd told myself it would mark the occasion if we had something at the church. Didn't want her to go as quickly as that. For the kids, too, it was better, it was more proper. As we were leaving the cemetery a young lad, the son of one of the guys from the branch, stopped me. He apologized for showing up late, but the traffic had been slow once he was off the motorway. He offered me a cigarette. Gillou had already gone back with Jacky. Fus hadn't left my side throughout the whole of the ceremony, filled with sadness, pierced by the day. Seeing that we were chain-smoking, he had ended up sitting on the stone bench down the far end

of the cemetery. He saw the gravediggers busying themselves around *la moman*'s grave so that they could finish
before nightfall. I was with the young lad at the end of
the graveyard where there was still room for three whole
rows, a nice leafy corner overlooking the valley, a lovely
spot, just a shame it was so close to all that death. We
talked about all kinds of things. I knew the others were
waiting for me at the bar for the coffee and brioches that
I'd ordered the day before. But I was enjoying smoking
with this young lad as if everything was fine. Relieved
that the day was over, glad that nothing had happened.
What was I afraid of? What could happen on the day
of a funeral? Relieved nonetheless. Filled with empty
thoughts, the questions, as useless as they were indis-
pensable, that would structure my days from now on.
What was I going to feed them tonight? What were we
doing on Sunday? Where did we keep our winter things?

FOR WEEKS WE were invited to Jacky's and to other people's houses too. We'd never had so many invitations in the three years of illness, or even before. It was nice, but it made me feel sorry for *la moman*. She hadn't been able to take advantage of any of that, of those endless drinks and snacks that led so nicely into a good meal. We got pretty drunk quite quickly so that we didn't have to talk, or else so that the flood of words came more easily. The most important was to break that awkward moment that would inevitably come. Feeling obliged to talk about *la moman* in a lower voice so that the kids carried on playing and didn't listen. Saying what we'd already said before, rinsing ourselves all out again. A blank as we waited for the alcohol to take effect, saying the happier things all over again, some nonsense off the telly, a good joke we'd heard the day before, finishing on a happy note because it was time to run. After that there were the summer holidays when people had pretty much gone away. I'd put Fus and Gillou down for football training in Luxembourg. We were camping in Grevenmacher, near the Moselle. I took them along in the morning, watched the first hour's training, then disappeared into the forests around the place. When I was brave I would go out on the bike, but since *la moman*'s illness I had this premonition, don't get knocked down, the kids would be better off with somebody to look after them. The campsite was nicely looked after, full of Germans doing the wine route. It was "good morning," "good evening" with them, and the three of us just enjoyed our own company. The kids told me about how the football had gone, how they'd got out of difficult situations, attackers on one side, victims on the other, with them right in the middle. There were clans in the gathering. The Luxos, French ones from Metz, the ones from Thionville and thereabouts. There was a lot of friction, and the little ones like Gillou took the consequences. Sometimes there was scrapping, and Fus threw punches when they picked on his little brother. They'd always been fond of each other, but since *la moman*'s death it was different. We took our time. They were both tired after their day, but we stayed together for a long time, sipping from our glasses, smiling at each other, sometimes looking at the other tables of people at the campsite. We drew up lists together, our favorite meals, the ten best all-time players of Français de Metz. Our biggest anxieties, our biggest laughs. *La moman* inevitably came up in conversation over and over again. The time she slipped on the spaghetti. All three of us remember it was the day Eurovision was on. We'd decided to eat in front of the television and she'd been in a hurry not to miss the beginning of the broadcast, and up in the air she went and the pot of spaghetti bolognaise with her. We'd spent a good half-hour cleaning up, the four of us. Gillou had asked us if she might be cross with us for laughing at her. We'd reassured him. She would have been happy just to see us enjoying the evening. Then my two rascals enjoyed stripping the story down, all the details, how she had slipped. They got up, they mimed her movements, her foot going right up into the air. What she said as she fell, the pasta, all the places we'd found it afterwards. They were handsome, those two boys of mine, sitting at that campsite table, Fus already tall and slim, Gillou still podgy, a round ball taking his time to grow up. They were sitting with their backs to the Moselle, and I had the loveliest view in the world in front of me. My eye ran from the banks of the river, almost sunk in darkness, to their alert open faces lit by our hurricane lamp. I was happy that evening and all the evenings after. I took advantage of that time. *La moman* had passed three months previously, I had shaken off my anxiety of not coping, of not doing all the organizing that I needed to do, all the things that needed managing. All the things that I'd already glimpsed for three years. It was a terrible thing to say, but it was almost easier now that there was no more hospital to deal with, all those evenings and Sundays spent waiting. Almost easier. If she had heard me. And yet it's true, and the holidays had never really deserved the name. A number of times I'd taken the boys for a bite to eat in Luxembourg town. We'd walked along the ramparts, then gone to a little restaurant where we spent hours waiting, there were so many people, and the kids had got impatient they were so hungry, but it made the huge steaks and the fat chips, each one almost a quarter of a potato, all the better. A fortnight of true happiness. Until there was the regret for not having done it sooner, when *la moman* was still there, but it's true that she wasn't too keen on camping, she preferred going to the South, "but not your SNCF railwaymen's holiday camp, OK?," so we only went every other year, we were on a budget, and there was the kitchen to do, then the balcony. We'd stopped going after she fell ill, which makes it more than three years ago. I'd made my mind a blank, all I had to do was take the boys to training in the morning and pick them up at four on the dot, I had the rest of the day to myself. I'd been surprised when I saw a colleague from the depot show up a few days before the end of the holidays. They knew I was there, they needed people for a cable that was threatening to drop and no one knew why. "It's well paid, all double time, the boss owes you that." "I've got the kids, it's the end of their course tomorrow, they get a little certificate, and they get a tournament as well, I can't do that to them." Fus was wiser than me: "Don't worry, the prizes at the end are made of tin, and I think Gillou's had enough of the Luxos, you know, they haven't been that nice to him, so it's probably just as well if we leave tonight." So we'd folded up our tents in a deluge. We couldn't see a thing, we struggled to get all our stuff packed away properly, and we'd ended up putting Gillou in the car for shelter while Fus and I tried to save anything we could. On the way home, at fifty kilometers an hour, in the middle of the great geysers thrown up by the car, I had taken advantage of the last few minutes of the holiday to promise myself to do that again every year. But the year after that we didn't go. Not because we didn't want to. It was because Gillou broke his leg a few weeks before. I didn't want to make him go camping on top of that. We had our holidays in front of the telly. It was the year of the Olympics. We'd spent our nights and mornings watching the broadcasts. Fus imitated the commentator Patrick Chêne, and Gillou the other one, Nelson Monfort. It was a fine summer when we slept from late afternoon – about five, after the last finals – till midnight or one in the morning to recover. We gorged ourselves on images, but then we would meet up again at night, all three of us, worshippers of the box, eager to see if the rubbish French medal counter was finally going to get moving. We were excited about everything, so long as there was a trinket to be won.

THEN THE TIME came when Fus wanted to go off with his mates, first Montpellier, and Spain the year after that. I didn't really know his pals, they never called by at the house but as far as I could tell I didn't much care for them. They weren't local, they came to the village on motorbikes, small-cylinder machines that must have cost an arm and a leg, and I didn't know where they got hold of that money. I didn't like their clothes either. I'd never been too keen on combat gear. But I didn't dare say as much to Fus, and when they went off to Spain I managed to scrape together a decent sum of money for him, so that he didn't need to be ashamed of himself and sponge off the others. After the holiday, when he began his final year, Fus had started seeing them every day. No girls at first. His results had almost got better. He'd been in the tech stream since first year, and the marks he was getting weren't that bad. It was almost a shame that he didn't carry on into senior high. What worried me was that he'd started talking to us less and less. It was only on Saturday morning, when we went shopping, that we still swapped a few words. On Sunday it was football and telly, and during the week he slipped into his room as soon as he could. He even spent less time with his brother, even though they adored each other. I didn't hear: "Fatboy, fancy a game of Magic? Fatboy, fancy practicing some free kicks?" as often as before. Gillou didn't seem worried, he kept on growing like a big teddy bear, and when I asked him if he'd noticed anything odd about his brother he said, "No, he's as funny as ever." And in fact I didn't find him amusing at all, my Fus. He wasn't the same. Even when *la moman* was reaching the end, he was less luminous than before. I watched him, all his gestures were gloomy, and on Sunday at football his tackles were harder, more vicious. Often he came back when Gillou and I were already at the table and he looked completely blank. "You're back from school at this time of the evening?" "No, I was with my mates. Fatboy, pass me a plate, please?" Gillou didn't just pass him the plate. He got up and went and served his brother. He piled up his dish beautifully with everything you could possibly have needed, like a waiter in a restaurant, then he went and heated it up in the microwave. Gillou had always done that. Serving his brother didn't seem to cause him the slightest problem, quite the contrary. I've always had this memory of Gillou looking radiant as soon as he saw his big brother coming home. A daily miracle. As soon as Fus had taken off his jacket, Gillou would talk him through the whole of his day in detail. He did that till he was fourteen. After that he was less voluble, but his pleasure at seeing his brother was just the same. Fus had always been more distant, but he did make the effort of giving him a word or two in return. Of course they had the odd scrap, more than once, but they were still a bloody beautiful pair. Life hadn't exactly showered me with gifts, but I had two strapping lads who liked each other. Whatever happened, each of them would always be there for the other.

After leaving school Fus had signed up for UIT, the University Institute of Technology. I don't know if *la moman* would have been pleased. It was the UIT, everybody told me that, but did they turn out engineers? Not sure. He'd have needed to knuckle down a bit more. I'm ashamed to say it, but when he got turned down by

Metz it was a real relief. I wasn't ready to see him go. He was doing all right at home. Even though he'd stopped talking to us that much, I needed him. Being on my own with Gillou had always scared me, I didn't think I was up to it. Too bad if the UIT was less prestigious.

24

THAT EVENING HE didn't get back particularly late from UIT. He was with us for dinner. He laid the table and heated up some wraps. That was their new habit. They didn't eat bread any more, and instead they ate wraps that they bought in packets of twenty and heated up in the microwave to soften them.

"What's that, Fus, your scarf?" Gillou asked him.

"No, Fatboy, that's not a scarf, it's a bandanna."

I took a look at the bandanna myself and I was puzzled.

"Fus, what's that cross on there?"

"Dad, I don't know anything about it, it's just a bandanna that a mate lent me."

"Fus, if you don't know then I'm going to tell you, it's a Celtic cross! A Celtic cross! My God, Fus, are you wearing fascist gear these days?"

"Dad, calm down, it's an ultra bandanna, not a fascist one. It comes from Lazio, from the Curva Nord. It's how they recognize each other. Bastien collects them."

Gillou watched our exchange in silence. Did he think the same as me? Did he also wonder if his brother was hanging out with a weird crowd? In the end Fus put the neckerchief in his pocket. We'd carried on quietly with the meal.

"Tomorrow after work I'm going up to the section, just eat without me."

They said to me, "Don't worry, it's all good."

They hadn't come with me for ages. When they were younger, before *la moman* fell ill, we all used to go leafleting together. We went off by bike, "a leaflet in every letterbox, if there are several names you put in as many as there are names, and if the box is already stuffed with papers don't put in anything at all, it's not worth it falling on the ground and people saying the Socialist Party are disgusting." Then the two of them would take one side of the road while I dealt with the other, they did it in relays, each doing a box in turn and pushing their pedals to make sure they got to the end of the street before I did. I heard them laughing or grumbling when the paper wouldn't go into the letterbox properly. When *la moman* became bedridden and I was exhausted from shuffling between the different doctors, they even did the distribution all on their own, like grown-ups.

I felt the need to go back to the section like other people need to go back to the church. Even if not much was happening, I told myself I'd be among the last. What made me sad was that we were getting more and more isolated. Unity on the left was long gone. Sometimes I had a sense that some of us were spending more time bashing the commies than fighting the rich. Where were our battles? We drooled over Lucienne's cake. I organized drinks with the communists from Villerupt. About twelve of them came, there were about seven or eight of us, and I had to get the car out and go and pick up the old ones who wouldn't have come otherwise. We had a glass or two, we said it couldn't go on like this, that we needed to make an effort to attract the youth, and at that moment everybody turned round to Jérémy, who was the only young person in the place, we sang "The Internationale," we kept it going to the fourth verse, the one about the people only wanting their due. Was there any point in it? I don't think so. I heard some distressing things that I didn't want to look into too closely. It had started with too many kebab shops in Villerupt, people wondering where the people were living. What was the problem? They weren't taking anybody's place, just some haberdasheries or knitwear shops where they'd never set foot. Would they rather have had broken and whitewashed shop windows? Those kebabs were a sign that people were still eating in the area. It attracts some weird wildlife, the other guy said, and also they're ugly, the one doesn't make up for the other, posters of mosques and those greasy tables below shitty neon lights. Yeah, maybe. Local people. People like you and me. Who would be happy to pay for something else, but who don't have much of a choice. I'd left Jérémy to deal with the guy, explain to him as nicely as possible that he was talking shit and that we might have better things to do than crawl up Le Pen's arse. "You want young people?" Jérémy asked him. "The kebab shops are full of them! You mightn't like the look of them, but believe me, those are the ones who are going to take us forward. Arabs or not." I'd always liked Jérémy, even when he was very young. He knew how to shake us up. He didn't take us for idiots, but he did know how to turn the hose on us when we got bogged down in slime. He has a gift, that one. I invited him for a drink after the others had gone.

Not at home. I didn't fancy the kids seeing us together. We met up in the Montana, in the backroom. We talked about the kebabs business, the moldy old remarks that our guys were coming out with and how we'd ended up here. I wanted to be intelligent. He seemed to be searching for his words as well. We didn't want to disappoint each other. He talked to me about his parents, who were turning into old fools. His father, most recently. They'd wondered about going back to the place they'd originally come from, but that had seemed an insurmountable task. The house was nearly paid for. They could survive on the dole and Jérémy's mother's salary as a teaching assistant for another few years, scared as they were. Jérémy asked me for news of Fus. He was hurt, that much was plain, not knowing anything about my son after all the afternoons that they'd spent together. When we, his parents, thought they would be friends for life. I sensed that he was feeling his way, perhaps he was thinking about *la moman*, how kind she was, and how delighted she had always been to welcome him into our house. Where had he been on the day of the funeral? Had he called Fus during the months leading up to that, or had they already fallen out long before? He couldn't remember. He couldn't name the day when their friendship had come to an end. All of a sudden he felt like a bit of a bastard. It must have made him miserable even at the time. Not enough to build bridges, just an itch. It was still Fus's fault, after all nobody had told him to get mixed up with that crowd. That evening, for the first time, he had understood that the whole business was more complicated. He turned his beer around on the old beermat and tried to align it perfectly with the logo. He told me that their friendship had slipped away from them. I hurried to say, "Yes, it happens. Don't beat yourself up over it."

The landlord came to our rescue. He started cleaning the tables, ours included. We were able to change the subject, start a new scene in a way. Jérémy talked about Paris and how he was going to study there next year. The way he talked about it, all at once and all over the place, it was as if he was ashamed, I made him start over. "Don't go so fast, we have all the time in the world, tell me everything, I'm interested." Then he gave me the grand tour. Sciences Po. The sweat to get in. The sons and daughters of posh families that he'd met in the corridors at his interview. The sensible route, spending the last year in Nancy to work with Germans. In the end he had decided to aim high and prepare for ENA, the

National School of Administration. Forty wretched places for the whole of France. "Do you want to be a government minister?" That was all I could find to say to him. I wasn't a match for this boy, the efforts he had just made to explain the subtleties of his career path. I was no better than those great lumps from just now. But Jérémy was nice. He'd continued: "Don't know about a minister. Maybe work in a ministerial office, why not, that's a possibility." That was Jérémy. He knew how to talk to the grassroots, not show them that he was too intelligent for their nonsense. He'd said to me with a smile, "I just have a rubbish first name for the stuff I want to do. It sounds a bit too fragile. With a Kevin, you know what the connotations are. You know what to expect. People know where they are with a Kevin who's daring to prepare for ENA. But Jérémy is nothing at all, it's neither one thing nor the other." I didn't know what to do, I'd never asked myself the question.

The evening wore on. The landlord kept moving about among the tables, filling the little ketchup bottles, putting back the salt and pepper. An infernal activity, a distracting movement. He watched us out of the corner of his eye, not being horrible, just taking an interest in everything that was happening in his establishment.

Jérémy talked to me about Paris again. The young people he had met there were wound up like clocks, full of ambition and certainty. He wasn't complaining, quite the reverse. He said to me: "That's what we're lacking here. People, starting with the teachers, to give us a kick up the arse. People to send us to Paris and not settle too easily for our modest successes. We're not worth less than the people I met there, except we don't really believe it. We don't even know that all of that exists." I didn't know if he was telling me all this because of Gillou. If Fus had missed the boat, it mightn't be too late for Gillou. We just needed to find the right moment.

The silence of the village kept us company. From time to time a car would pass along the riverbank, and we watched after it almost as far as Rédange. Nothing else. The landlord had switched the radio off and turned his dishwasher on in the kitchen. He was still listening in on us. His bistro, in spite of its name, in spite of the stupid red neon light, imitating an American diner, which took up the whole of the bar, was still in its original state, filled with bright white light, so white that it couldn't claim to be anything else. I'd only started coming back recently, when I was sure I'd be able to control myself and stick to my beer, sometimes two, never more. Besides, I only set foot in there when the evening was right, often after the section. Not necessarily to talk about things. Or to drone on. Not like some people. It was nice to come out with a clear head and not get straight back in the car: I carried on to the church, along the Chemin des Cantonniers, a small climb of almost a kilometer, much of it covered with ivy, and reached the cemetery, which is closed at that time of day. I talked to her quite loudly, I tried to tell her some nice thing I'd thought of. I talked to her about the children, about how they were growing. I imagined her being happy to know we were together.

Jérémy must have been aware that he was losing me. He stopped talking and said to me, "I'm also doing this for us, to make things change. I'll be more use there than here."

"I believe you, and even so you don't need to justify yourself for anything," I replied. And then I said, "I'd like Gillou to do what you're doing. Do you think you could have a word with him one of these days?" Jérémy had suggested that I bring him to his parents' house, I could see he wasn't ready to come back to ours, the place was still haunted. But he seemed happy with his mission, his first opportunity to play the leader role that he'd assigned himself.

Jérémy and Gillou spent several afternoons together. Jérémy gave him books and papers to read and introduced him to two of his mates from ENA prep, a boy and a girl who also came from the sticks, but who were already, just like Jérémy, ready to go. They were credible voices, all the more credible in that the girl that Gillou asked me to drive to the station was absolutely gorgeous. She was heading for Paris too, "but it's only a stopping-off point," she saw herself as going much further than that. In just a few minutes, on the way to the station, we'd talked about all kinds of things. She was the one who came up with the topics, like a young woman in a hurry. Gillou was in ecstasies. He listened to our game of verbal ping-pong, the clear opinions of this girl sitting on the back seat who had slipped into the space between the two front seats, her face between ours, putting her arms around us to avoid hitting the windscreen if I crashed. At the station, she disappeared with the words "So see you again in the capital?," this to Gillou, who hadn't had time to reply before she was off. That was Paris. We didn't say a word all the way home.

JÉRÉMY DID A good job: until Christmas, Gillou made a huge effort on all fronts. He'd talked to the teachers, we'd gone to Metz a few times, to Nancy, and even to Paris for the Lycée de Carnot open days, "a doorway, a demanding one but not insurmountable." In the entrance hall we were welcomed by old boys, Louis Aragon, Gustave Eiffel and plenty of others. Endless vitrines showing their old notebooks, exam papers and army passbooks. In among those little displays, a plaque in memory of Guy Môquet.[1] The rector's speech was held in a hall that had windows up to the ceiling, not especially beautiful, but so what, it was all about selling a better world. There was nothing to guarantee that there was a place there for my Gillou, and I had no way of helping him into it, so I just smiled shyly and stupidly at everybody, teachers, pupils, janitors, whoever we bumped into: my little contribution to his ambitions. Gillou, once he'd found himself a seat at a pavement cafe table, he said with a smile, "Let's not get carried away. I've got to make it through to the end of year and get decent grades." I took a look around the area, which oozed money, the perfect facades, all those well-dressed people busying themselves, and I'd wondered where we could find accommodation for Gillou in a place like this without having to sell the house. There weren't many places in halls, and I didn't get how they allocated the few available rooms. But Gillou was right, we still had a long way to go. We were both caught up in our thoughts. Gillou suddenly asked: "Do you think Fus is happy with all this?" I had no idea, probably not, I'd have thought. But I preferred not to think about it too much. "He'll always be proud of you, Gillou. You can invite him up to Paris for the weekend. Or you could come back. You don't have to pay for the train until you're twenty-five, so you can come back as often as you like." I didn't convince him. I wasn't convinced myself. But we stopped there. We spent the few hours we had to kill before the train in the Musée du Quai Branly, on Jérémy's recommendation.

Fus was pleased to see us. He'd cooked dinner and tidied the dining room. He listened to his brother's news, and gently teased "the Parisian." As soon as we were sat around the table, Gillou launched off, talking about his future life. He'd abandoned any kind of caution, as if he was already there. Why dampen his new enthusiasm? And yet I was superstitious. I kept saying, "We'll see, we'll see." Fus said "stylish," but did he really think that? It didn't stop Gillou, who was very excited. Fus fiddled with his glass, his knife and fork. The transfer window, as he called it, seemed to be coming into focus: his brother would be on the Paris bench next year and he'd be staying at home. I felt sorry for him, Gillou's careless babble had become unbearable to both of us. I suggested to everyone that they go to bed. A strange day that had left me miles from everything, buffeted around between a thousand contradictory thoughts, without the slightest idea what I was supposed to hope for.

IT WAS BERNARD from the section who alerted me. "Hey, have you got a sec? I need to tell you something. You know the comrades were out near the depot yesterday? We were sticking up posters for the first of May when we saw that gang from the FN at the end of the tracks. They were sticking up posters for their Joan of Arc thing, under the bridge and all along the wall that goes up to the switch. We snapped in, there weren't many of us, same as them, no better, no less tooled up than them. Nobody really wanted a scrap. Mimile and Ominetti had gone home already, and the rest of us weren't exactly tough guys. And since they didn't look all that much more committed than we were, we decided to shout a few insults and leave it at that. We spent another couple of hours slapping up our posters over theirs, and I imagine they've fucked with our work since then. That's life, what do you expect?" I didn't understand what he was getting at. It was a long time since I'd been out putting up posters, and that kind of thing went over my head these days. It was a game, to see who got the last word. Everybody had their own territory, places where only their colours were acceptable. You should have seen them, some mornings, when they'd invaded the other side's territory with their posters. "What bothered me," Bernard went on, "is that I think I saw Fus hanging with them. I wouldn't stake my life on it, but there was this big bloke who had the look of your son. The guys didn't notice, but I'm almost sure. A jacket with a big Apache on the back, is that him?" "Maybe, well, no, I don't think so," was all I could stammer. Bernard went on: "Don't beat yourself up, young people do stupid things. Just don't want him getting into trouble. You know how it is round here, there are some hard men who wouldn't think before whacking anyone, even your son." And thumping me on the arm: "Shame they're turning the kids' heads like that," he finished. Fus was twenty-five, he wasn't a kid. What was he doing hanging out with fascists?

When I asked him in the evening he said he didn't know anything. He'd just gone along with his pals, it was the first time they'd gone out sticking up posters, and he wanted to see what it was like. While I thought that evening through, wondering what I was going to do, slap him, have a fight with him, in the end nothing happened. Nothing at all. Nothing I could have imagined. I didn't have it in me to sort him out. That evening I felt incredibly cowardly, and very old as well. I remember looking out at the garden for a long time. It was really beautiful, the fruit trees were beaded with the thaw that had just begun, and an inky cloud said it was due to bucket down in half an hour or so. I should have gone back in and joined him, I'd prepared myself for a discussion, not even a bollocking. "How could you have done it?" I asked him. He just said, "It's not what you think." What could I have thought? And then he went on: "When did you stop putting up posters? When did you start just going for cake up at the section?" I'd asked him if he didn't feel awkward spending his time with racists. "They're not racists, that's the old days. Anyway, my mates aren't racist, any more than you and I are." "No, not racist, just against immigrants," I added. "Against immigration, Dad, not against immigrants. The ones already here don't bother them as long as they don't mess things up." Normal people, in short. And then, as if determined to convince me, he said again: "They're good guys. Not like you think." He had sat down at the end of the table. Perhaps he was waiting for me to join him, to go and grab a couple of cans that we could both neck down. I stayed in my corner, near the window, behind him. Keeping an eye out to see if Gillou was on his way back. Worried that he would find us like that. Fus went on talking softly: "Believe me, these guys are on the side of the workers, you'd have been together twenty years ago. They don't care what people say in Paris. They're only interested in this part of the world, they don't want to see it die. They're moving. They've had it to there with all the European crap. They get their cash from Paris and they redistribute it round here. Last Saturday, for example, after a poor old man got burgled, they fitted out his house from top to bottom. Like it or not, these guys aren't exactly spitting on people." That's how you justified hanging out with the far right in less than ten minutes. How you resigned yourself to your son being on the other side. Not the side of Macron, but of the very worst bastards. The mates of Holocaust deniers, absolute scum. Fus was calm, almost contented, that this explanation had hit home. He assumed. A real Jehovah's Witness, head stuffed with nonsense, new certainties, and still lovable. I was ashamed. We were going to have to live with it from now on, that was the most awkward thing. Whatever we did, whatever we might have wanted, it was done: my son had knocked about with fascists. And from what I could tell, he'd enjoyed it. We were in one hell of a mess. *La moman* could be proud of me. In the end Fus got up and said, "It doesn't change anything."

IN ALL THE weeks that followed, I didn't go out except to work. I avoided bumping into him, but it wasn't always possible, and then there was Gillou. We behaved ourselves over meals. We avoided starting debates. It was Gillou who did it in our place. We still agreed on plenty of things. Wondering how it's possible. How could he love what we had always loved, when he was hanging out with fascists? He kept on humming *la moman*'s favorite Jean Ferrat songs,[2] as he had done since her death. Christ's sake, did he understand the words? "Desnos leaving Compiègne to fulfill his own prophecy." How could he go on singing that song? Now he was hanging about with the same people who'd bunged the poet on the train. And yet I didn't say a word. Just once I asked him to be quiet, Gillou looked at me and smiled at his brother, a wink, "the old boy isn't in a great mood tonight." Luckily Gillou didn't understand. All the better.

My thoughts kept turning back to it. And yet, as he had said, it didn't change anything. I went to see him at the stadium. When he went out with his gang, he did it discreetly, as if he wanted to avoid hurting me any more. He had a certain regard for his stupid old dad. There were even long weeks when he stayed at home to revise for his end-of-year exams. I'd hoped for a while that it was over, that one evening he'd say, "I don't know what I was thinking," and come back to me. A moment of pure relief. Going up to the section together. To visit the grave of great-uncle Laurent, CGT member[3] from the very beginning and deported, buried under red and tricolor flags. But that's not what happened. Quite the reverse, he started going out again.

One time a guy from the gang rang the bell. I opened the door to him. Nice face. Normally dressed. Very polite. I brought him in, we exchanged a few words, because it would have been hard to do otherwise. I even think we shook hands. Mechanically. He complimented me on the garden, said it was his parents' hobby, and that he sometimes gave them a hand. What could I do? Now that I'd let him in, now that we'd talked a bit, I wasn't going to have a row with him. I wasn't going to run away either. Fus had taken some time to leave his room. I looked at him again. A healthy, athletic fellow. Open expression, lots of character. Not nasty-looking at all. The type of guy you'd wish your kids would have as a friend. At last Fus showed up. They both spent ages saying goodbye to me, two good mates. They left arm in arm. They got into a little chrome van, probably hired.

Throughout the day I'd thought of that guy time and again. I'd tried to imagine him chasing after Arabs at night and beating them up. But it didn't work. Not for my son either. But they must have done things together. Fascist things. Otherwise what was the point? However much I struggled, none of it stuck. It all slipped away from his angelic face.

When Fus came back that night, contrary to his usual habits, he didn't go up to his bedroom, he came and joined me in the kitchen. "That was Hugo," he said, "His parents live in one of the houses near the Beller stream." As if that was supposed to put my mind at rest. Little workers' houses, most of them done up, not far from the railway station. I didn't know anyone there since Armand sold his to a couple of young nurses. "They're nice, you should see their garden . . ." "I know, your pal told me,"

I interrupted. Fus just said, "Ah, fine, good." I set about furiously grating carrots, which kept my head down in the salad bowl. Between the desire to go on talking, to find out more about this fellow Hugo, about what they'd done that afternoon and not dropping the face I'd been putting on for him for several weeks. He stood beside me for a long time in silence, stiff as a plank. He was waiting for me to open up, which I didn't that evening. Then he started emptying the dishwasher, complaining that it had stopped washing anything properly, which wasn't completely untrue, but I'd been avoiding that expense for months, and after hand-washing what needed to be washed, conscientiously wiping away any lingering scraps and putting everything away nice and clean, he finally had a good reason to cut short our session and leave the kitchen. For my part, I had the feeling I'd already done a lot, and I was pleased that we could live together without hitting each other.

He and his guy Hugo and some others collected old furniture locally, wardrobes, heavy black antique cupboards which they refurbished to sell on. After stripping them down and giving them a good wax, they made them bearable. Or else they painted them in the colors that people like these days, taupe, bright green. Most of

them went like hot cakes, and the stinkers that found
no takers went straight to the poor. I knew all that from
Gillou, who followed his brother's exploits from a
distance. They seemed to have a good laugh on Facebook.
You saw them stripped to the waist working away at their
planks. The studio was a total tip, beer bottles all over
the place, tags on the wall that were hard to read. Some
of them had cigarettes in their mouths. With long hair
and ponytails, they wouldn't have been out of place at
one of our youth clubs in the old days. Now it was more
of a short-back-and-sides look. There were two or three
girls in the pictures, and they looked almost scary. They
didn't seem to do much in the workshop, just watched
the guys doing their stuff, sitting on a work bench, big
Doc Martens on their feet, army trousers, men's tank tops.
Their faces were filled with arrogance and hatred. And
if only it had stopped there! The page went on to say
things about rap music that I didn't get, but then there
were a bunch of comments in which they fucked and
bollocked anything that wasn't certified as pure white.
Jews and queers got the worst treatment, followed closely
by Arabs, but like all the rest it was accompanied by a
long sequence of little smileys, so I shouldn't imagine any
of it led to anything of any consequence. Every now and

again, some messages asked them to rein it in a bit, moderators or little local bosses who didn't want Paris whacking them over the knuckles, but the whole thing was revolting. So Gillou was aware of what his bro was up to, and I'd been naive to imagine that I was protecting him from all this. "So you know?" I asked him. "Yeah, but it doesn't change anything," he answered simply. He was another one, then. I was the only one who found anything to object to. "Nothing about this shit shocks you, it doesn't bother you that your brother's involved in it all? Does that mean you think the same as him?" "Dad, Fus isn't like that. His mates are a bit wacko, but he's still sound. And since they've been doing their restoration work I don't think it's been all that bad. No one forces them to do it, and it takes up their Saturdays. They're better off doing that than hanging around in the local bars." "But don't you feel like telling him he's messing up?" I pressed. Gillou just said, as he often did, "Chill." I don't know what faith he was relying on, how he imagined the return of the prodigal son. "Chill."

We moved on to the next stage and it stayed like that for several weeks. Apart from his studio, and when the weather permitted, Fus camped with his mates about ten kilometers away from us in quite a nice neck of the woods. A farmer had – under what sort of pressure I don't know – let them have a tiny plot with a cabin on it that they used as an HQ. They'd put up tents all around it, reinforced with planks and canvas. I regularly consulted their Facebook page, without Gillou's help. And I saw the same faces. Their thing looked like a squat. As in all squats, nice things grew surrounded by shit. They'd built a beautiful veranda where they had their drinks. Gillou had said to me, "You see, they don't care about politics, what interests them is doing that kind of thing, hanging out." And it's true that just looking at those photographs, and if you bleeped out all the rest, if you didn't read the disgusting comments that their page was stuffed with, you could have imagined that everything was fine.

THE TUESDAY AFTER Whitsun Gillou got the replies to his various applications. He came down from his room and said, "It's sorted." "What's sorted?" I asked him because I'd forgotten all about the date of the results, and I'd been focused on his *baccalauréat* tests. "It's sorted for next year. I've got all my choices. Lycée Fabert with boarding. Carnot in Paris too, but I'm on the waiting list for their boarding. Far down the list, so I don't think I'll get it," he went on. "Shitty of them to do that. To give you a place and let you find your own accommodation. They shouldn't be allowed to do that for guys from the provinces. Anyway, I think I'm going to confirm Fabert, Metz is fine." I nearly agreed and was inches from saying, "Do what you think's best," but it was Fus who saved my skin: "Don't be an idiot, Fatboy," he told him, "aim high! If you've got the chance of Paris, take Paris. Dad and I will sort you out a place to live." I looked at Fus and I had to leave the room, because I was misting up. A tide surged over my head, my eardrums thundered, great round teardrops like globes formed and broke. I cried my heart out in the car, and then again on a bench at the cemetery. Not even close to the grave, but that didn't matter, I felt OK there. When I was sure I could stand it, I held my face under the tap that they'd set up at the end of the cemetery, no one ever knew why. A little old woman who looked after the flowers on the graves had been giving me sidelong glances. I must have startled her, with my puffy face and wet hair, and yet I think we knew each other from a distance. I was scared about going home. But nothing had changed. We had a peaceful evening, Fus and I got back into that fake rhythm where we said only the bare minimum when talking to each other. That evening I asked Gillou, "All good? You've confirmed Paris?" He just said, "Yes, thanks."

That month it had been incredibly windy. Gales and heavy rain, lashing the whole region, bringing everything low. Fus had come home, when their campsite had been completely inundated. One morning he said to me, "We need to sort out a room for Gillou in Paris. We ought to get it done before the holidays, because once term gets going it'll be too late, there'll be nothing left." He was right, but I kept putting it off. I'd vaguely thought about the railwaymen's hostels, without really doing anything about booking anything. Fus went on: "I can go there with him this week, if you want. I've got a mate we can stay with on Saturday night. If we go through all the ads we should be able to find something." I didn't reply to Fus, because I'd stopped talking to him. In cases like this I usually just got on with things, often taking his advice without acknowledging it. It happened quite naturally. That's how things were now. He talked to me, he told me what he had to tell me or ask me, ideally in front of Gillou so that the conversation, if there had to be a conversation, wasn't kept just between the two of us. And I did what I had to do. If I didn't understand, or needed to check on something, I found a way of mentioning it to Gillou so that he would talk about it to his brother. Or else I didn't do anything and let the situation rot.

And anyway I let them go. It was the first weekend after the exams. I gave them everything they needed to reassure a landlord – wage slips, testimonies from the railway, even a statement from the bank account that *la moman* had opened just before she fell ill, and which I'd scrupulously paid into since then, as if it was the most sacred of duties. They came back empty-handed. And set off again the following weekend. And so on until mid-July. I asked Gillou if I needed to come, and they answered: "Don't worry, we'll get there in the end." They wore their best clothes, clean-shaven and hair neatly combed. Two fine young men. I wondered who this pal who was putting them up every Saturday might be. Gillou, when I grilled him, was very vague on the matter and told me he'd barely even seen him. He enjoyed these trips away with his brother. Even without finding a place to stay he came back radiant on Sunday evening. Fus was just as jovial. As if he'd forgotten we were on bad terms, he talked to me as soon as he got home and told me everything in detail. I let him get on with it and didn't ask him any questions. Then, after a few minutes, he realized what was happening, remembered where we were with each other and switched off. I only found out later that the guy whose place they were staying at was a fascist, a guy who was up to his ears in the Front National. It was Gillou who gave it away after they'd found a place for the start of term. Fus had put terrible pressure on him not to say a word. They'd been sleeping in that room that was also a store for posters and baseball bats. Once again the only thing I could think of doing was shout at him. I was in a fury, but my fists refused to join in, the blows disappeared into the void, as if in a nightmare. Twenty times I saw Fus's face, his neck, his big Adam's apple quivering away, twenty times I wanted to grab him, I knew what needed to be done, where to put my hands, grab both sides of his T-shirt and bring them sharply together, snapping the collar, use the fabric to choke him while at the same time bringing my knee up into his balls to pin him against the wall, it was all possible, I knew how to do all that, and I'd done it to others in the past, but nothing had come, my arms dangled feebly. All of my rage stayed in my head, ran down my throat, heated up my lungs, but it went nowhere. On the contrary, my legs were like cotton wool and my arms completely pointless and frozen. Then I yelled my head off, I could still manage to do that. I yelled at him never again to mix his little brother up in his stupid affairs, I yelled at him that he didn't deserve his mother, I yelled all kinds of other deranged things, the vilest things I could think of. He looked at me, not quite believing his ears. But not challenging me either. Almost worried for me. When I'd run out of breath and vileness and insults he just said, "It was hard to do otherwise, do you see that? At least we found him a room. Not too expensive and not far from his school." Then, so as not to slink away like a coward, he checked that all my rage was spent, that I wasn't about to tear into him again, before leaving the room. I hadn't said a word to Gillou. Even though I was angry, I couldn't open up another battlefront with him. What good would it have done? And it was true, the room in Paris had been sorted out, and that was more than nothing.

Fus didn't hold it against Gillou for spilling the beans to me. On the contrary, he was very much caught up in what was happening in Paris and as the days passed he brought him loads of things that would be useful to him once he got there. A standard lamp, a lovely desk lamp, more crockery than he would have known what to do with. They were always real presents, expensive brands, bought at the Terville department store and paid for with his apprentice's wages. He had also brought him clothes, with jeans and fashionable T-shirts: "You don't want to look like a hick in your class of champions. Fatboy, you're representing Lorraine, promise me you won't fuck up from now on. You can save your fat-clown jogging pants and your supermarket sweaters for the weekend." My rage against Fus hadn't subsided. I steered clear of all this exuberance. Sometimes I wondered whether the excess of gifts wasn't really intended for me, as a way of winning me over. Gillou, subtler by nature, was good at sparing my feelings and saved the bulk of his thanks for when he was alone with his brother.

AUGUST IS THE best month in our neck of the woods. The mirabelle season. The light at about five in the afternoon is the prettiest you'll see all year. Golden, strong, sweet and yet filled with freshness. Already with a hint of autumn, run through with streaks of green and blue. That light is what we are. It's beautiful, but it doesn't stick around, it's already heralding what comes next. It contains within it something that's not so good, the days that will quickly pass and grow chill. Indian summers are rare in Lorraine. You often hear people talking about the summer light in northern Italy, and I'm willing to believe it, I've never been, but I'm still willing to bet that ours, during that very brief period, those two weeks right at the end of the summer, at that precise time of day, far surpasses it. The light of the last outdoor aperitifs. Jacky and his wife kept inviting us over. "See, we haven't seen you with the kids all summer. Are you pissed off or something?" I did everything I could to wriggle out of going, I'd been so ashamed. But Jacky kept insisting. What could I do? He had always helped us, he had always been there when things were serious. I took advantage of Fus and Gillou's absence one night to go over. "You've come on your own?" he asked me. "Well yeah, it's a bit complicated with the kids. They say hi." "I've put on too big a spread, then. I got a ton of ribs for them. Never mind, you take what's left and they'll still taste good tomorrow. They'll be even better, in fact." Jacky had spent some time as a hospital cook. Food at his house always came in huge quantities. He'd built himself an enormous barbecue that could take a whole pig. It took him an hour to get the thing fired up, and when he did it consumed a whole bag of charcoal every time. Sitting on their terrace made me feel a lot better. Getting a slightly different perspective on things. His rockery wasn't that bad in the end. When, two years before, he had got rid of his lovely flower beds, "too much maintenance, you know?," I hadn't understood. He'd spent whole Saturdays looking for Jura hole stones in the nearby hills, finally he got lucky, and I gave him a hand carrying them. Some of them, the ones that supported the whole structure, must have weighed a good fifty kilos apiece. He'd almost ruined his car filling it up over and over again. In spite of all his efforts to organize his little hillock I still wasn't convinced. Before, his hydrangeas gave him flowers all year round, and now there were only unhealthy-looking flowers that he had delivered and which yielded nothing. Expensive things that came from all over the place, and which quickly perished. Since then, thistles and dandelions had taken over the middle of the rockery. A thistle is a fine thing when you look at it properly. It's full of surprises, no two the same, unappealing body but a lovely face.

Since I felt as if I was wearing Fus's story on my face, I told them everything, quickly, to get it out of the way. As I told them everything I was aware that I didn't even know which way they voted. We'd never talked about it. I'd always assumed they were on the left, but I'd never bumped into them up at the section or on any kind of demo. He was a man of the people. She was the same, even though she'd finished senior high. No airs. Their parents were local too. They'd worked in the factory, they weren't farmers. And even though he'd taken evening classes and trained as a chef, Jacky, for me, was still a worker. It was possible that the two of them weren't that far from the FN. In any case, they hadn't been too shocked by my revelations. "Fus will always be Fus. He's a good kid," he said to me. Then he'd come out with some sort of nonsense about how the FN wasn't necessarily wrong about everything. But not quite as clearly as that. Getting himself lost in meandering sentences along the lines of "careful I'm not saying that . . ." mixed with others, "don't imagine for a second that . . ." I didn't want to dig too deep, I didn't know if the intention was to put me at ease about my son or whether he sincerely thought those thugs had access to a kind of truth. It wasn't the evening to make a fuss, and then in any case night had fallen quite quickly and we'd moved on to other things as it invited us to do.

AT THE START of September we'd had to fix Gillou up at his place in Paris. I hadn't been able to imagine myself doing the trip with Fus, and all three of us in Gillou's bedroom. So the two of us had set off, Gillou and me, the car all loaded up. Loaded so full that the question of Fus coming along didn't even arise. But I knew, and the boys knew too, that in other times we'd have managed. At worst we'd have suggested that Fus take the train and meet up with us in Paris. The idea had crossed my mind, it was so long since the three of us had been together anywhere else but at home, but with the best will in the world it was impossible, completely impossible. All the same, Gillou could have begged me, but he didn't. We set off like that. Fus kissed his brother as if it was perfectly normal, then he stayed near Gillou's

65

door. Pretended to run beside the car like Charlie Chaplin when I started the engine. Gillou only had eyes for him, but as soon as we'd got past our street he immersed himself in new thoughts. I watched Fus in the rearview mirror even after the car was passing through the little avenue of detached houses, past the end of the village. I could still see my son, standing up straight, saying goodbye to his brother, without a rebuke for anyone. Understanding and accepting that that was how it was, he'd stayed affable from early that morning when we'd started packing all the things together, maybe hoping that I'd change my mind, all the way to the pavement where he'd done his best not to spoil the party. There was nothing to stop me turning round, chucking out all the luggage on the back seat, finding a new and better way of organizing it, and the three of us setting off, but I carried on driving, in more and more of a hurry to get to the motorway. It was once we were on the A4 and a good twenty minutes past the toll gate that I said to myself, "There we are, it's done." And then, "How shitty it is. What a truly shitty life."

I'D BEEN APPREHENSIVE about September and meeting Fus face to face during the week. It was agreed that Gillou would come home every Saturday afternoon and we'd take him to the station on Sunday evening so that he was ready for anything on Monday morning. In spite of the distance, that was possible now that there was the TGV. When Gillou came back, not until three on the dot because he had to do four hours of monitored homework on Saturday morning, there were two of us fighting over him. Fus didn't go out until he'd seen his brother, and we made him tell us everything in the course of an hour. Since Fus and I hadn't really spoken to each other all week, we were both more than happy with all this excitement, hearing Gillou's resonant voice filling the room at last. The subjects were inexhaustible, and kept us busy for both weekend meals, because it was all over by Sunday evening, we didn't have supper together, and I made him sandwiches to eat on the train.

Gillou had soon admitted that he was swotting. It occurred to me to invite Jérémy to the rescue: after all, he must have made the same journey. Jérémy, like Gillou, had been coming home every weekend since the start of term, and often they took the same train. When Fus saw Jérémy in the house, it was as if I'd finally found a way to finish him off and make him pay for all his nonsense. The two former best friends gave each other minimal greetings. Jérémy hurried to sit down at the dining-room table and open his files. He'd brought lots of photocopies which he organized and commented on, holding them out to Gillou, who was glued to him, drinking in his words. Fus and I soon felt superfluous. Fus had tried to stay and listen to what his old mate was saying, but since Jérémy was only interested in his brother he was sidelined. I heard him starting up his moped like a fifteen-year-old. This time with a good reason to set off and see his henchmen. I went on inviting Jérémy over on Saturdays at exactly five o'clock. Jérémy and Gillou worked together. They swapped tips, in only one direction at first, but I was even pleased to notice that my

Gillou was getting to know a few things. Jérémy finally agreed to have a bite to eat at ours. First of all he went on talking about his studies, about Paris. The things to see and do up there. Fus put up with it to the best of his ability. He even tried to take an interest and asked a few questions whenever he could. The other two answered him, there wasn't a problem there, but if he hadn't been there it wouldn't have made any difference.

Every other Saturday we headed off for the match in Metz. Football, whether it was Fus playing or FC Metz, was still neutral territory. We still went there together. We went on celebrating our team's goals. I just avoided standing next to Fus, which stopped me jumping into his arms when our attackers scored, and in fact if that had happened it wouldn't have been so bad, Fus understood as I did that it didn't mean anything, that exceptional moments of hysteria didn't change everything else. Our Senegalese players could still line up the goals, the shaven-headed deity, Renaud, could light up the field, and we were still where we were: two guys who barely talked to each other anymore, if at all. We always went to the same stand, the one overlooking the canal, which had always been the cheapest one. I remember that in the old days it wasn't even covered. So above the goal and the Horda Frenetik, or what was left of it: it had been dissolved the previous year because some cocky idiot chucked a firecracker at the Lyonnais keeper. The Horda tended to be mostly people from our side, or mine at least. If it was fascists you were after you had to go to the other side, to the Autoroute stand. The two stands exchanged insults every now and again, clashing when they had to share the visitors' car park, sad old story. Still nothing like what might have been happening in Paris. Jérémy came with us when he could, even though football had never really been his thing. I enjoyed buying his ticket and standing him a beer at the end of the game. As with the meals the four of us had, I was surrounded by these three guys, and in spite of the business with Fus, that was still something. I still had a sense of keeping things under control in a way, so that everything didn't fall apart completely. *La moman* lived within me at such moments; I think she was happy with the way I was handling everything. I told myself she would have done much the same. And besides, I hoped Jérémy might make Fus rethink his ideas.

Once the subject of Paris was exhausted, we had to talk about something else. Jérémy didn't know about Fus, at any rate I hadn't said a word to him. As soon as he got back to Paris for the new term, Jérémy had gone to the Rue de Solférino to meet the Socialist Youth movement, who had tasked him exploring new forms of solidarity. I couldn't really tell what that meant, and neither could he, from what he told us, but every now and again it brought him into contact with the big cheeses, people you saw on TV. Jérémy's role was to understand how youth movements get organized, when there were fewer young people in political associations than there used to be. Jérémy told us that one Saturday evening. He grew passionate about micro-organizations that recruited on the internet. Ten or twelve guys, groups as ephemeral as butterflies. No nonsense, genuine participatory democracy, practical actions decided on in the morning and put into effect in the afternoon. Heaven in Jérémy's eyes. He couldn't stop talking about it. But if there was a heaven, it meant there was also a hell. And Jérémy started in on young people who strayed – in greater numbers than you would have thought – into movements more or less closely affiliated to the far right. They too were abandoning the big guns and turning towards small local groups that were all different from each other but saturated with the same violence. Opting for the pleasures of the moment, from underground cage-fighting competitions to neo-Nazi concerts. For Jérémy they were the worst, the damned of the damned. "Compared to them, the Front Youth Movement or GUD[4] are a bunch of civil servants." Fus had been listening. He was good at listening. He'd always been good at it. He never interrupted whoever was speaking, in fact he prompted him to keep going with a look. Even when the other person stopped to get his breath back or clear his throat, Fus didn't cut in. That evening Jérémy hadn't stopped. He talked to us for a good hour about the "fascistosphere," as they'd started calling it on TV. Gillou watched for his brother's reaction, which wasn't forthcoming. Fus had just started clearing the table, with the food scrapings on the top plate, the knives nice and clean and crossed under the forks as *la moman* had taught him. He did it carefully so as not to interrupt Jérémy, and kept his eyes on him throughout the whole maneuver. He only got up when the whole talk seemed to be over, and once again he took an incredible amount of time to do it, ready to sit down again if Jérémy had something else to add. He came back with some beers, saying: "That's all Parisian nonsense. It has nothing to do with us." He deposited his cargo of bottles on the table, then went off to find some snacks. The conversation had moved on to something else when he came back with the corn puffs that he and his brother ate at all times of day, even and especially after meals. Gillou must have talked to Jérémy afterwards and told him about his brother, because the topic of the far right never came up again.

WE MANAGED TO live like that, knowing what we did, as best we could. Two of us during the week, four at the weekend. During the week, Fus and I dodged around one another, we spoke to each other without words. We did what needed to be done, respecting the few points that were needed if we were to be able to carry on living. Like being at work during the bad years: good morning, good evening, the tasks required for the proper running of the house, "when you go out, leave the key at Jacky's, he's coming to pick up the tools tomorrow," "I'll do the shopping this evening" (but never again "anything particular you'd like?"). Fus's "don't wait for me this evening" came as a relief and allowed me to gain an extra day before the weekend, even if I felt a bit of an idiot with my plate wedged on my lap in front of the TV. It was like being in the theater: we kept our distance, gauged our entrances and exits so that we were never stuck in the hall at the same time. Gone were the days when we crammed together around the little basin in the bathroom to brush our teeth. Gone were the days when the three of us did the washing up at the same time, on top of each other, constantly getting in each other's way, touching and gently jostling each other. Now our movements were heavy and cautious: we had to leave a good margin, if possible let each other out of a room before we entered it. As if we were wearing a one-ton protective suit and walking into some hellish radioactive zone.

But my fury was passing. I knew it, but I didn't want to hear it. I talked to *la moman* in the evening. She saw me and her big lad haunting the house, but I didn't hear her asking me to forgive and forget, I really didn't. Otherwise I would have changed. Like me, she couldn't shake things off. Like me, her fury subsided, but not her shame. It wasn't the eyes of others, as I thought at first: the ones who knew didn't seem all that shocked. None of the things I had feared had happened. I had a different son and people seemed to be able to deal with that. Or they pretended they could. Fus wasn't an addict, he wasn't some fuckup who terrorized the district, and that was enough for people. They knew now that he was different. They were just careful about what they said to me, careful not to hurt me with some stupid observation, a bit as if I'd told them Fus was gay. So nothing particularly bad. It required a bit of attention, but it didn't go anywhere.

In the end we had Jérémy at ours almost every week. I enjoyed hearing him tell us about his studies, almost as much as I enjoyed hearing my Gillou. When I wasn't off on a job I proudly went and picked both of them up at Metz station so that they could avoid having to make a mid-afternoon connection. Waiting for the local train could be a real pain every other Saturday, I was well aware. And even when the connection to Thionville happened without a hitch, the journey took a good hour and a half, almost as long as Paris–Metz. It was a lot quicker by car. It was our little ritual, I set off good and early so as not to make them lose a single minute of their precious free time. I'd made them something to eat that I would keep till the evening, chicken wraps, some crisps and drinking yogurt, stuff they could have on top of whatever they'd already eaten on the train. I wanted them to tell me all about their week, but I sensed that Gillou preferred to wait until we got home and for

Fus to be there before he started talking. I respected that, so we put on the radio, a book program that we liked well enough, not too highfalutin, with some Canadians speaking with an incredible accent. I think Jérémy liked seeing me, seeing the boys – even with Fus that awkward moment seemed to have gone, they'd found a rhythm – and coming to ours as much as he could. There was a lot of arguing at his parents' house, about nothing at all and also, from what I could make out, about more serious matters. If we hadn't been there he would have ended up cancelling his season ticket and staying in Paris. These trips became my new life. I felt I was doing something deeply useful, my backside crammed into the seat, my sciatica lying in wait, ready to attack as soon as I made a wrong movement, and me managing to keep it at bay throughout the whole of the journey, concentrating on my route, because the A31 rarely gave much quarter: either you got through or it finished you off. Making those trips was my contribution, however small, however derisory, to those two lads' success.

Even in mid-afternoon, as soon as the season turned cold the journey got difficult. The stretch past Thionville lost none of its beauty, but it did get more serious.

More closed. And more slippery. We knew we'd had it for a few months, and we were already keeping an eye out for the first snows. We started paying attention to certain bends in the road. We weren't unhappy to make it home. Usually, Fus was there, busy tinkering in the garage to catch Gillou as soon as he got out of the car. A dog wouldn't have been more faithful. On that first Saturday in November, he wasn't there. We missed that look of fake surprise that he gave us when we showed up, as if he hadn't already been pacing about the garage for a good half-hour waiting for us. We'd dropped Jérémy at his place just before. We'd arranged to meet up later, to grab a bite and head up to Metz for the game. We found Fus lying on the sofa, with his face demolished. He only had one eye. The whole left side of his face was nothing but one great wound, blue, black, swollen – it would have made you throw up. He looked at us, in a total daze. As if he was dead. There were paper towels everywhere, drenched in blood. And it went on dripping from behind his ear. His left arm, curled in front of his chest, was trembling away. So were his legs. And we just stood there, for endless seconds, still knackered from the journey, startled to see this strapping fellow completely shattered. At last Gillou ran to his brother. Fus just yelled, "Wait!" before he collided with him and broke what was left of his ribs. It took us an incredible amount of time to get him into the car. At the wheel, emotionally wiped out, I drove like a man possessed.

I WAS STRESSED out by the journey, because I couldn't remember where the emergency entrance was and as far as I could recall it wasn't easy, there was something unexpected about it, a turn-off that you couldn't afford to miss without having to drive round in circles for five minutes. I was angry with myself for not remembering. I'd always been good at remembering places, it was worth doing. Fus was groaning on the back seat. A horrible business. I kept an eye on him in the rearview mirror, he really looked worrying. Partly the road, partly the mirror and obviously as a result I missed the sodding turn-off. As we didn't have time and I was in a panic I took the first no-entry so as not have to go round again. Arriving in front of the hospital I had the same amount of trouble dragging Fus out of the car as I'd had getting him in there with Gillou. In the end we'd put him on the back seat, sideways on, his legs resting on the front seat, which we'd bent forwards towards the windscreen. Fus was like a zombie and didn't help us. He just groaned like a frightened animal as soon as we tried to touch him. Gillou spoke to him constantly, trying to encourage him to go with it a bit, but Fus was powerless, incapable of moving even slightly. Outside the hospital it was even worse. Gillou had stayed at home because there was no room in the car. And I couldn't do it on my own, with the best will in the world. I parked like a fucker and blocked the firemen's entrance, and some orderlies eventually showed up, yelling at me to get the fuck out. They weren't afraid of Fus's cries. They grabbed him in a rush, as they had to. One of them said, almost with a smile, "At least we're not going to need the chainsaw!" As soon as he was out of the car Fus fainted. The two guys swore and ran inside with him. Once they'd got that out of the way they bit my head off. What was I thinking of, bringing him in myself? In cases like this you always call 15, the emergency number. The lesson went on and they said over and over what they'd already said. 15, 15, 15. After that it was the hospital and I was all too familiar with that. Waiting, the people in overalls walking past without a word, and sometimes with a pinched little smile for no one in particular. I hadn't yet had time to think about anything. I'd done everything automatically. The automatic reflex of an old man, wheezy as all hell, but then again having my son's life in danger had put years on me. I would have as much time as I liked to think about what came next, the aftereffects and everything that was going to change. Gillou kept ringing and I had nothing to tell him. I was too groggy to come up with platitudes. He wept on the phone. Me too, I think. I saw my Fus as a cripple. I saw him sick forever. Because we're all a bit dumb that way I thought about football and I told myself that he wouldn't be able to play the next day, as if that was the most serious thing. When they told me he'd been put in an induced coma I threw my guts up. I vomited standing up, no spasms, all at once, still looking at the doctor. His gold-rimmed glasses, his face, not particularly worried but not reassuring either, the face of a specialist who wasn't about to commit himself, who had seen too much to risk any kind of prognosis at this stage, the face of a stranger. We would wait till the next day to find out more. The doctors told me to go home, I was useless there and nothing was going to happen during the night. I knew that, I didn't believe in the power of the mind – or at least not there, not like that – and I basically had no hope of giving anything at all to my son, whom I hadn't addressed three words to in weeks, but I was too knackered to go home, I'd have ended up in a ditch. So I stayed in my car, on the back seat, like Fus a few hours before. I saw the lights down below, where they'd put him. For a few moments I looked at the shadows behind the frosted glass before plunging into a coma of my own. It was *la moman* who woke me up. I felt like an idiot for sleeping so much. I ran to the hospital as if there was a bus to catch or something. Fus was still in his coma and his swellings had barely gone down. It was too soon. You've got to be patient in hospital. The whole of the rest of the day had been in keeping with that. No one knew. There was something they didn't like, I knew, they didn't need to tell me. Gillou turned up with Jacky. And they picked up Jérémy on the way. Jacky asked me what had happened but I hadn't a clue. Gillou must have told him already. He didn't press the point. After those few words, no one tried to talk. Every now and again, if our eyes happened to meet, Jacky said, "It'll be fine." A bit like a mantra. "He's a tough one, our Fus." Softly, almost to himself. There was no point saying anything more than that. We occupied the four seats of the little waiting room just outside the two big doors to the resus room. There was nothing to do apart from look at the posters about hepatitis prevention that we must all have read about a hundred times. Jacky was breathing hard. I told him a few times he should go home. He said, "Are you nuts?" In spite of our efforts not to move, not to get in the way any more than we had to, the air was stale. And the people stared as they passed. A bunch of parasitic thoughts filled my head. I thought about Gillou and Jérémy's train, about how they mustn't miss it − I'd counted it down in my head. We still had plenty of time, but it had started to bother me. I didn't know if they had their things with them or if we needed to call at the house. I didn't dare ask them, I didn't want them to think I was a moron. Only having that to worry about. Having nothing better to think about than a son in a coma. We were still in that little hutch when the cops arrived. They asked if we were the family of Frédéric Schmaltz . . . and they trashed the rest of our surname, even though it's a perfectly good Lorraine name. I said, "Yes, I'm his father." "In that case," they said, "we're going to have some questions to ask you." I don't know who had called them, presumably the hospital. They wanted to know who'd messed him up like that and the fact that that was how I'd found him didn't prove my innocence in their eyes. They asked me what I'd done that morning before going to Metz. What they didn't like was that I'd taken Fus to hospital myself. "I wasn't going to let him lose all his blood without doing a thing!" I told them. "Quite, sir, there are emergency services for that, so ideally you call 15." Bloody 15. I didn't have good memories of 15. Once for *la moman* we'd waited for 15 for ages. Couldn't they understand that I hadn't thought for more than a second? "So who was it?" they asked me in the end. And I hadn't a clue. I hadn't thought about it for a second after finding Fus.

IN THE END Fus got out of hospital four days after he was admitted. Nobody wanted to give a diagnosis of his eye. He had lost three-quarters of his sight in it. There was nothing to suggest that it wouldn't get better, but it was also likely that it would stay the way it was. His eye barely moved. It didn't look like an eye, more like something dead. A tar-covered bird. His left arm was messed up too. There too, the trouble he had lifting it and moving it might only have been temporary, but the doctors didn't want to paint life any prettier than it was.

Fus had been questioned by the police and at first he'd said he didn't know. Since it was impossible that he knew nothing, that he couldn't say anything, they'd pressed the point. Then he'd said, "I was with my girl-friend. They couldn't stand us. We'd already had run-ins with them. Antifas. I couldn't tell you exactly where they came from, but I think they're from Villerupt. A bunch of them set on us." If we were talking about the same ones, these were some guys I knew from a distance, some guys who were too extreme to stand alongside us, but who I'd shared a few battles with. They were guys who'd had a rough time of it over the past ten years. They couldn't stand anybody, not teachers, not socialists and not even the French Communist Party. They weren't anarchists either, or Workers' Struggle, just people who went round picking up causes of one kind or another, mostly quite local but often with a few Germans or Luxos in there as well. A funny mixture. No agenda. Sometimes they would meet up to go to a concert or cause trouble on the edge of a demo. It had to be them. They weren't from the section, and they weren't from the union. The cops pushed Fus to press charges. And every time they asked me to try to persuade him. Things between us would have had to get back to normal for that to happen. And they hadn't.

THERE WAS SO much to get back, so much to recover. Since Fus came home I hadn't had time to think, I'd just gone on taking care of everything at a great rush, checking that he had all the medication he needed, that the nurse – and it couldn't be just any old nurse, I'd had a lot of trouble finding one – came to treat his eye every day. According to the doctors, his skull had taken a horrible bashing and there was still the possibility that there'd be some kind of aftershock to come, so I kept an eye on all his reactions. How he spoke, how he walked. How he ate. And he ate quite weirdly, he drooled a bit, his swallowing was a bit painful, but it was hard to tell if it was his arm that was giving him trouble or if it was a bigger problem. I blew my top when Gillou wanted to stay. I didn't want him to pay for his brother's stupidity.

I think he didn't get what I was on about and I scared him when I said, "God Almighty, Gillou, don't get involved in that, you have your own life to lead! Don't mess it up with all this nonsense." He said, "He's still my brother," but that didn't seem enough for me. Since the hospital I'd been focused on the absolute bottom line, where there were no questions to ask. Treating him and nothing more. I couldn't see myself leaving that role, which suited me. When you didn't find yourself wondering every five minutes if it was worth seeing your son messed up like that, if it wasn't time to stop our nonsense given the scale of events. I hadn't got there yet. And looking after him, as if I was looking after a wounded animal, gave me the attitude that I needed. No fury about my son having been damaged, no wish to hunt those guys down and finish them off, I'd leave that stuff to the cops. The whole subdivision had shown up around our place, including the ones you didn't usually see, who wouldn't have shown up if they hadn't noticed the stream of people going in and out of the house. There was something rural about this procession of people, and I imagine that back in the day when someone kicked the bucket, when he had his arm ripped off by a machine, that's how it went. All of them, Jacky first and foremost, were urging me to find those bastards. And my lack of interest in the issue had nothing to do with my convictions, I couldn't have cared less if those lads got in trouble with the law. I had no special sympathy for them. But I found it hard to imagine that Fus hadn't had anything to do with what had happened. But devoting myself completely to his health and forgetting everything else struck me as a sound compromise. With Fus I rediscovered the words from childhood, "Are you OK?," "Does it hurt when I press on it?," and he replied in fragments like a sick and exhausted little boy. His friend Hugo came. He was the only member of the gang to show up. "I wasn't there, I really don't know what happened," he hurried to tell me, as if I'd asked him a question. Fus hadn't woken up for Hugo any more than he had for the other visitors, he remained mute, almost as if he was mentally disabled, more sensitive to the weather – he grunted when it rained, groaned when the end of the day looked bad – than he was to people. Only Gillou, when he came on Saturday, managed to drag him out of his lethargy a little, but it was almost nothing compared to the effort he put into it. Still, Gillou clung, as I did, to that almost-nothing.

THE COURTROOM WAS full. The press had done a good job. The lawyer hadn't managed to relocate the trial, so it was held in Metz. I knew the court from outside, it was on our way when we were coming back from the stadium and grabbed a bite to eat in Place Saint-Jacques. An imposing building in Jaumont stone, which looked great at every time of year. Summer and autumn suited it best, but now, in winter, it was already a fine, almost acid shade of yellow. The surrounding area was empty. The square was free of cars, kept away by the snow, with Mont Saint-Quentin in the distance. It was chilly, but it was still a fine day. I slept in a nearby cheap hotel – nothing in Metz was really very far or very expensive. At reception, when I told them I was taking a room for at least a week, they asked me if I was there for "the" trial. Yes, I was there for the trial. The one for my son.

I turned up early. The lawyer had told me he would help me, but I hadn't seen him. He probably had better things to be getting on with. I found the courtroom easily. I'd been told that the first hearing wouldn't do much apart from choosing the members of the jury. As they were chosen at random by the judge, I assessed them: for or against Fus? The lawyers, on either side, were quicker than me: some potential jurors who had just been called, and who had just stated their names, were dismissed.

Fus watched this game of ping-pong without a word. He had put on the blue jacket that suited him, he had a clean white shirt, at any rate that's what it looked like. His hair was short, but not too short. I think the lawyer must have given him some advice; not a good idea to look like a Nazi. Now he looked more like a student looking for his first trainee position, like so many I saw showing up at SNCF. The two policemen on either side of him didn't look mean, I think they were used to it and didn't see the point in aggravating matters. Fus looked pathetic in the dock, so alone, so gaunt and ravaged, a shadow in this huge blond-wood room. He wouldn't move as the days passed. I hadn't seen him for several weeks, I hadn't been able to. The first visit in prison was enough for me. I hadn't said a word at visiting time. Neither had he. I could have told him of the enormous shame I was experiencing, that he had caused, that I wanted to forget him and act as if he had never existed. For whole nights I had tried to erase him from my memories, but he went on dancing in front of me, happy and bare-chested, arms around his brother, emerging from our little rubber pool, that little circle two meters across, a horrible-looking thing that had kept them both busy for whole summers. Afterwards I saw him showing off at the dinner table. He was catapulting the water bottle cap at his brother. The shouts and annoyance that followed, because he was cheating, because he was spilling water, because the cap always ended up where it wasn't supposed to be. He came with me to hospital, I saw him as a well-behaved young boy, a devoted athlete who came to me for a consoling hug after we lost a match. I tried to carve out the bits I wanted from all that, to find that lost child and reformat my memories. Too bad if it meant sacrificing some lovely moments, too bad if I had to lose a bit of everyone else. But he was everywhere. Without him, what was I left with? Youthful memories with *la moman* before he was born? So vague that they barely came alive. Gillou all on his own? Not so many pictures there. However deeply I dug, I couldn't see any memorable ones. Fus filled my life. And now he had to disappear. The sounds, the smells of prison went with me at all times. Here too, in this room, I saw him in the dock and I imagined him in the morning, getting ready as best he could, shitting in front of his cell-mates, trying to make himself presentable for the court. But he must have smelled terrible, his last shower must have been the day before, maybe two days. I was disgusted by his condition as an inmate, a prisoner, a jailbird. All those words repelled me, with their rancid smell. If he'd run away I could almost have borne it. If I'd known he was on the run, somewhere else, why not, I would have had to accept what he had done. It wouldn't have done too much damage to what we'd been through together, but like this, in jail, I couldn't, he dragged us all into his sodding prison, at every moment of our lives.

At first, the trial was constantly being interrupted, like an engine that needed breaking in. I took advantage of those pauses to go outside, to go back down towards the Moselle. To go to the Protestant church, see the playground of the Lycée Fabert. There were few things that still gave me strength. Strolling about near that school several times a day was part of it. All those young people who were also taking the air. Some of them were pulling odd faces; the morning checks mightn't have gone the way they wanted. I wanted to tell them. I wanted to tell them that it didn't really matter, it didn't matter at all. And even at the very end, for the ones who flunked their year, who failed their *baccalauréat*, it was still OK. Nobody had died. They wouldn't be spending tonight in jail. Are we always responsible for what happens to us? I wasn't asking myself the question for Fus, but for me too. I didn't think I deserved all that, but maybe that was just a notion, maybe I deserved everything that was happening to me and I hadn't done what needed to be done.

I got up very early. And every time I did it was the same thing: I had a moment's reprieve, just a moment, long enough to emerge from my dreams and nightmares and pack away my night. As soon as I worked out that I was at the hotel, the whole trial came crashing down on top of me. I was surprised to see that my nights still resisted Fus and weren't filled by the events of the day. I still had pleasant moments, often quite eccentric, but no different from the kind of dreams I'd always had. Even the nightmares were still bearable, no worse than before, they were about missed trains, endless running. Inconsequential fears. I was walking on mountaintops, I could have fallen at any moment, but I kept going in the wind and eventually I let go. Not very serious. It was even reassuring to know that there was a territory with a logic of its own, a little kingdom free of the vileness of life. Maybe that was telling me how things would be afterwards, and well, if that was it, it wasn't so bad.

Returning to the day, for a few minutes I contemplated the room, where there was nothing but the trial: the dark suit that I aired as best I could so that it would do me for ten days, no book, I was unable to read anything at all, no music either. What might a person have read at such a moment? Just my trial clothes, a flask of instant coffee and some medication. A bit of TV to dull the mind in the evening. At reception they had lent me a kettle and my meals stopped at Cup a Soups and Pot Noodles. Sometimes they sent me up a salad or some leftover cake. Things left over from the buffet and which were going to go off anyway if somebody didn't eat them. On the advice of my lawyer I had booked the room under a different name. Maybe they thought I was from the victim's family? Maybe they didn't care? The trial made a lot of noise, but for most people it was just a minor news item. One that they would forget in a few days if they hadn't done so already. Only a few of us had been battered into the ground by it. The guy that Fus had killed, first of all, his family and then the three of us.

THE INDICTMENT WAS clear. It was murder. The investigating magistrate had insisted on premeditation and, in spite of all the efforts of Fus's lawyers to query that during the legal instructions, it was on that basis that the trial was conducted. The sentence for manslaughter was ten years, twenty at the most. But for that the two would have had to have met by chance and fought until one of them had succumbed to the blows. When you had kept watch on the guy for several days, when you waited until he was on his own to show up with a bloody great iron bar and whack him from behind, several times, until you'd smashed in half of his skull, that was called murder, and that meant life. Saying that, some might have thought me cynical. Not a bit. When they read out the indictment every phrase resonated in the depths of my bones. A branding with a red-hot iron wouldn't have felt more real. I can still hear each of the words, each intonation, and then that silence, that huge silence that followed, as if it had taken the whole world by surprise. As if until that second nobody had known why they were there. I had quickly lost the thread since the first few days. I couldn't tell what they were looking for. That search for detail, for the tiniest little thing, struck me as pointless and artificial, as if they had to justify the roles they were playing and their salaries. The doctors were the worst. I'd soon had enough of their caution. They couldn't state with certainty that death had been caused by the blows. My God, what did they need? When they screened the photographs of the guy's skull, you could see that it wasn't normal, that you couldn't easily go on living with half your head looking like a peeled grapefruit. But the worst were the witnesses called by Fus's lawyer, who couldn't bring themselves to focus on the thrashing that Fus had taken, who couldn't make the connection between the beating he'd taken and the one he had dished out several weeks later. However much Fus's lawyer tried to press them, they remained vague. In any case, did that excuse anything at all? I wasn't convinced. "It isn't a matter of excusing, but of highlighting the field of attenuating circumstances," the lawyer had explained to me. "Any circumstances that might significantly reduce the sentence." I didn't give a damn what sentence Fus was going to get, I had no interest in discussing the number of years he was going to spend inside. It would be a lot. A hell of a lot, and I knew I would be dead before he got out one day. He deserved no better. On the evening of the second day, the lawyer asked to see me to prepare my testimony for the next day. From the beginning, he really didn't get me, I knew that. My reactions weren't right. I hadn't followed him in his bid to dismiss any idea of premeditation, I hadn't been much help to him in demonstrating the damage that Fus had suffered, in setting out how his life since his attack had been drained of everything, how that huge shock had knocked him sufficiently off balance to make him take his revenge. "A father does that for his son," he said to me. Perhaps. For my part, I was ready to set out how things were, what Fus had been until the end of his teenage years, the most lovable of children, the lovely kind of child that you would wish any parent to have. I was ready to say that he came with me to hospital without a word of complaint. I was ready to say that, because it was the truth, the simple truth. But when the lawyer wanted me to talk about his mother, say how

fragile her death had left him, I didn't know anything
about it, and it was asking a lot to put poor *la moman*
into this story. I didn't know if *la moman* agreed with
the idea of acting as an excuse for her son the murderer.

Since the beginning, I had been apprehensive about
the moment when I was going to be called, and I started
sweating from every pore. The more I thought about it,
the more it dripped. Panicking, I looked for handker-
chiefs, or anything else, but I had nothing. My light
blue shirt was drenched within a few seconds. Whatever
I tried to do, pulling my jacket in all directions to hide
the black sweat patches, however much I tried to rear-
range myself, it was all you could see. Luckily there was
still a while before I had to stand up, and after struggling
for a long time, halting my breath, halting everything I
could, focusing on the first judge advocate, I managed
to calm myself down.

I couldn't look at the judge, I couldn't look at Fus. The
judge advocate remained a good point of orientation; I
studied him, I saw how he tensed at certain phrases, and
sometimes how he relaxed in his chair. He seemed to me
to be in line with what I had in my head: for me justice,
harsh but impartial, this guy, always clean-shaven – he
must have had a quick go with the razor every time there

was a break in proceedings, at least the one at lunchtime – with his half-moon glasses that he was constantly adjusting. His eyes were fixed on the room, reading everything that was happening. When he looked at Fus, he really looked, as I would doubtless have done if he hadn't been my son. Sometimes his gaze swept the jury, waking some of them up with a lieutenant's glare, or calming them when the discussion got heated. This man could have worked anywhere as long as there were people listening to him and doing what he said. He could have been in the armed forces – I could easily have imagined him in a submarine – or he could have been in charge of a thousand steelworkers, he had the stare for it. It was a long time since anyone had impressed me like that. Compared to him the hospital big shots, and even the head of my depot who was still pretty impressive, all six foot five of him and with that huge mutt that never left his side, all those guys who knew how to shut us up, all of them, as many as there were, still had a lot to learn. I wondered if my lieutenant's parents were still alive, if they sometimes still came to check up on their son. I hoped they did, they could have been incredibly proud of him.

On the other side of the judge was a woman. A pretty redhead, in her forties, who looked as if she was bored out of her mind. It had been so long since I had looked at another woman that I got no more from her than that. I guessed she had other concerns and was only waiting for one thing, for the hearing to come an end at last. But after Fus there was a rape case, so the magistrates and the jury still had another good three weeks to go. When she returned to the trial, you could see – and it didn't take hours to notice – that she didn't like Fus, it was as obvious as a cobblestone striking a cop's face. She really didn't like him. Unlike the two others, when she'd finally suppressed the unimaginable quantity of yawns that were constantly assailing her, she often took notes, lots of them at a time, her head really bent over her papers, with a certain level of agitation, as if she was as afraid of missing something, but perhaps in the end it wasn't anything, just a way of escaping her irresistible desire to go to sleep.

In giving testimony, I would be obliged to see Jacky, still sitting three rows behind me, straight-backed on his bench. Jacky had put on his tie. He must have taken leave of absence. I don't know why he was inflicting that on me. There was no sign of him during breaks in the hearing, or indeed in the evening. By the time I went outside he had gone. I was annoyed to have him peering over my shoulder like that, I didn't know who he was doing it for. Maybe it was just to check that I wasn't mucking about too much with his Fus.

When they called me to the witness box I couldn't remember how to walk, I didn't know how the murderer's father was supposed to behave, what could "decently" be expected of him. I'd imagined I could make myself even smaller than I was. Show that I had nothing to do with any of it, tell them that my son was a grown-up, he was no longer a minor and he was fully vaccinated, and that he had acted alone against my will. Tell them in no uncertain terms that not once had I encouraged him to take his revenge, the idea hadn't even come into my head. My testimony was an important moment in the trial, as they said in the *Républicain Lorrain*. It would crystallize a lot of things, and Fus's lawyer had invested a lot in it. And since I'd had trouble coming up with good answers he'd eased off on me, he'd asked me why the boy had been on his own so much, why I'd abandoned him so often to his fate. He seemed to know so much about our life, he had reminded me of things I'd forgotten about and put them in perspective, a horrible perspective that made me look like a neglectful and abusive father. And the more he put me down the more

I'd begun to doubt, to reflect that there must be an element of truth in it all. He had been particularly insistent about my political commitment. Without really saying as much, but strongly implying it, it was as if I'd driven him straight into the arms of the FN. According to him I was, if not responsible, at least the primer for what had happened. I emerged demolished. I ran to the exit to avoid meeting anybody. A young woman stopped me before I made it to my refuge, the Moselle. "What he did is normal," she said to me. "It's to reduce the charges against your son, any good lawyer would have acted in the same way." Under her arm she had a big book stuffed with notes, probably a law student who had come to learn about real life. I didn't know what to say. The lawyer had destroyed me with his insinuations. She went on: "You're not risking anything. You won't go to prison because you left your son alone at home from time to time. On the other hand, it might win your son a few years, so it will have been worth it, don't you think?" "That's not really what happened," I bridled, "I've always been with my children, as much as I've been able to . . ." "It doesn't matter what you've done or haven't done," she cut in, "the main thing is the story that the jury will have in their heads when they have to make their decision. The important thing is to chip away at their initial vision, the one that leads inevitably to thirty years' imprisonment. It's to break down their prejudices, sow some doubt in their minds. A lot of doubt. The more they doubt, the more they'll sweat and that, believe me, is a good thing. It'll bring the sentence tumbling down. When you have doubts, you would have to be a total bastard to sentence somebody to thirty years in prison. It happens, unfortunately, but it's rare." The next day it was the turn of Jacky and others who had played alongside Fus at the football club. I think Fus's lawyer must have been satisfied. Fus came out of it as someone quiet and winning. Someone reliable, a master of his emotions. They all seemed deeply convinced by what they were saying. But the best thing, the strongest thing, was Jacky who said, "I know it might seem unbelievable, given where we are today, but Fus" – he had a hell of a lot of trouble calling him Frédéric and was pulled up by the judge several times – "is the son I would always have liked to have. And my wife, who is in the court, could tell you exactly the same thing. I don't know what you're going to decide, that's not my business, but I can't help thinking that our Fus is a good kid who's never had that much luck." That caused a stir in the courtroom. When he had said that, Jacky had turned towards me, as if to say, "You see, you bastard? That's how you defend your son." Of course he'd been countered by the plaintiff's lawyer, on the grounds that Fus hung out with a far-right group, that the death hadn't just happened out of nowhere, that there'd been a few blows from an iron bar, all the things we knew already. Jacky had stuck to what he had to say: "All of that may be true, I'm not going to tell you anything that isn't, I'm just saying that our Fus, Frédéric, that is, is a good kid who doesn't deserve this."

The next day I met Krystyna, Fus's girlfriend. She was a strange girl. She'd chosen to turn up dressed entirely in black. She wore a crepe blouse from another time. You could see tattoos at the edges of her sleeve and her collar. A lot of tattoos. Still, with her glasses and her ponytail, she looked like a model pupil. I found it really strange meeting this girl at last. I couldn't help looking at her the way a father observes his future daughter-in-law the first time they meet. I conscientiously examined her and wondered several times if I liked her, if I could see her with my Fus, as if all of that made the slightest bit of sense at this juncture. As if they had the slightest chance of living together one day. She was from a Polish family who'd settled in Moselle between the wars. She had been a militant supporter of the FN since the age of fourteen, "like my dad." It was always fascinating to see how people could feel like stakeholders in a country's history, more French than the French, their houses still crammed with the religious knickknacks and traditions of their country of origin, and with the same ardor and the same obstinacy, how they refused a similar right to the people who came after them. Krystyna had talked in detail about her meeting with Fus, she had explained how he wasn't like the other members of the gang, he was calmer, simply nice, "gallant" with the girls. That made the judge sit up. She had to confirm what she had said: "Yes, gallant, your honor. That's how he is. Frédéric was attentive in a way that the others weren't. He was a lot less macho than they were." She'd gone on to explain that Fus was often childlike, and that the others saw him as a bit of a softy. On the day he was attacked, she'd been with him. It was just the two of them, but yes, you couldn't have missed them, she was carrying tracts by Marine Le Pen right there in her hands. Four or five of the guys had approached them, she couldn't remember exactly, and grabbed the pamphlets off her. Fus had taken a step to get between them and taken a beating. It had all happened very quickly. As soon as she'd screamed they disappeared. They hadn't talked much in the weeks that followed, because Fus had almost stopped saying anything at all. At that moment in her statement, Krystyna turned towards Fus. She stopped for a few minutes to look at him and smile at him. Fus immediately lowered his head. Then she went on speaking to the jury: she set about persuading the other members of the group that they had to do something, that they had to respond. Go and beat them up in turn. She recognized at least one of the guys in question and knew where he hung out. The one with the pock-marked face. The one who would die a few weeks later under Fus's blows. But for now the group were well behaved. They decided to go back to Marine's strong-armed men in Thionville and talk about what to do. In the meantime it was urgent that they didn't do anything. She yelled at them, then she came to cry at our house. She told Fus that those bastards could sleep soundly at night, that no one in the gang was willing to avenge him. Fus just said, "Leave it." She could have sworn it was the only thing he said that afternoon. "Leave it." And that she didn't understand how Fus could have done that. What it was that made him make his mind up. That everyone else was to blame. That the whole business could have been sorted out between men in the way that they were sometimes able to do, with just a few punches thrown, group against group, nothing more than that. Yes, she was angry with her gang for leaving Fus to take his own revenge. And it was understandable that things had degenerated. The judge picked her up on that phrase, but the idea was there, and everyone in the room understood.

THAT DIDN'T STOP the sentence from being harsh, when it was delivered two days later. Twenty-five years. There was some applause in the court. Not a lot, but enough to make me even more disgusted. Fus stayed inert throughout the whole of the judge's reading of the sentence. He didn't even give a start when the twenty-five years was announced. Krystyna uttered a cry of rage and pain. That made me feel odd, when I hadn't flinched and hadn't even looked at Fus. The lawyer came to see me: "You've got to appeal. Your son hasn't benefitted from any mitigating circumstance. Twenty-five years is pretty steep." I didn't know what to say, I didn't know the price of a man's life. That night I calculated the date when my son would get out, January 2045. It seemed unreal, and yet that was what had been uttered, that was what had gone on record. I got a sense that not everyone was horrified by the sentence. I wasn't in a hurry to get home. I'd taken the room for the night and went to bed asking them not to bring me up anything or knock on the door. Then, on the stroke of two, it occurred to me that there was no sense in locking myself away like that. I grabbed my things. The only person at reception was the night porter. He let me leave without a word. I imagine he looked at his register and saw that everything had been paid for so I could do what I liked. Once I was on the road, there was a chance of ending up in a ditch, but I didn't take it too seriously. I just drove very fast, taking a swig every now and again on the bad whisky I'd bought at the service station. "We're not allowed to sell it at this time of night," he told me, but I handed him the notes and he backed down – and let fate decide on things for me. Jérémy and Gillou were waiting for me at home. They hadn't gone to bed. Jérémy was looking after Gillou, who had been drinking as well, "to keep him from doing anything stupid."

I QUICKLY WORKED out that getting drunk for whole days at a time wouldn't get me anywhere. I'd done the same thing after the death of *la moman*, and come out of it again. I didn't want to go diving into all that again. But I still wasn't fit for work, and the SNCF doctor understood that. He warned me straight away: "We can't put you up there again. You're going to have to wait a bit." I didn't want to contradict him. I too felt that walking about on the overhead wires could be a danger given the thoughts that were running through my mind; I couldn't concentrate on anything, particularly not on any kind of safety instruction. I couldn't see a future for myself, and wasn't keen on the idea of burning my arm off with some clumsy maneuver. The doctor was relieved that I agreed with him, I had colleagues who were furious when they lost their jobs as cable fitters because it also meant losing the risk and penalty premiums that went with them. To be frank, I couldn't see myself working on the ground either. And the doctor had seen that too: "We're going to leave you on your own for a bit, if you promise not to get too desocialized," he said to me. I reassured him and thanked him for the few weeks off he gave me. He was a severe kind of guy, who didn't have a reputation for handing out presents, something of a skinflint according to my colleagues, which made the decision all the more unarguable. No danger of my bosses checking up on me to make sure I wasn't swinging the lead as long as it came from him. Besides, I could go out as much as I wanted, "it was even recommended for what I had." The relief at not having to go straight back to work. It was the doctor's decision, and the fact he had made it so quickly, that had finally convinced me that I was in a bad way.

AT OTHER TIMES I might have taken advantage of those free weeks off to do a couple of jobs about the house, but this time it wasn't possible. There was Fus's room, which haunted me and stopped me from doing anything. I didn't know what to do with it. Empty it completely. Or wall it up. I passed by outside a few times without being able to go in. The door was half-open. You could make out just about everything at the end of the bed. Strips of bandages and compresses left over from his last night in the house. Bottles of disinfectant. If he'd been dead, I would definitely have thrown myself on his bed and sniffed his scent one last time. Sat down and looked from his bed, his room, his football cups. Spent a long time studying the books he had kept. Collections that he hadn't read for years, but which were still neatly arranged on his shelf. Books that had survived the passing of time, knowing nothing about what had happened. But he was rotting in jail, it wasn't the same thing. Gillou, when he came back, didn't feel the same revulsion. He popped into his brother's room from time to time. Motionless at first, scrutinizing every object. Then he cleaned it, as if Fus was going to come home the next day. He sorted through his things: "He never wears that, maybe we could give it away." And as I didn't say anything, he conscientiously folded up the clothes that he'd outgrown, putting them in big kit bags. "Give them to the charity shop." I would have had to have the courage to go there. I knew they would happily accept all these things, and they wouldn't ask where they came from, but that still didn't persuade me. It was all too much. I wore my son's imprisonment on my face. The lawyer kept calling me immediately after the trial. First of all it was just short messages: "Please call me back," and then, when I didn't return all his calls, he let rip. A long plea in which he said it wasn't in his interest to put on pressure and spend more time on this case – he had reminded me in his halting and fretful message that his fees were covered only by the legal aid we'd applied for, so that wasn't going to bring him in any money – but that wasn't the issue, he still had to do it. He repeated it several times. In every available tone. "A simple matter of justice." He added that it was up to me to persuade my son, and that we didn't have an eternity to do it. I didn't want to. Any more than I wanted to visit him in prison.

It was Gillou and Jérémy who assumed the task of persuading Fus to ask for an appeal. They both understood and weren't angry with me. They managed on their own. I think Jacky went with them once or twice. Maybe I'd have done the same if it had been Jacky's son. Maybe it was easier when it wasn't your own son, you could show magnanimity, you didn't feel stained by prison. Yes, perhaps I too would have liked to be a visitor. You kept your hands clean. But in this case it was my son. Everything that happened to him happened to me. And for that reason I had chosen to keep my distance. I wasn't feeling that strong and I'll always be grateful to Gillou and Jérémy for never rebuking me, and never forcing me to do anything. They suggested that I go and live in Paris for a while. They would arrange for me to stay at theirs. Jérémy's flat was big enough, and the two of us could live there for a while without treading on each other's toes. I didn't want to. Paris would remain a sanctuary, watertight enough and removed from everything that had happened to us. No one in Paris had heard of the trial and it was better that way. On the contrary, I would have preferred that my two boys stayed there, that they didn't go to all the visiting rooms, but that was too much to ask. They hurried to prison as soon as they could. Gillou didn't tell me anything about it. Jérémy was more expansive. He asked me if I wanted any news from Fus. Because I didn't reply he started telling me anyway. Gently, with a lot of careful phrasing. We'd lived like that for several weeks during which all memory of the time before was banished, when every word was weighed. I pretended to be concerned about their studies, but deep down I knew that that was broken too. That nothing now, yes, nothing that could happen could bring me any degree of pride or satisfaction. And Gillou, in spite of all that he could have done, couldn't do anything about it, that's just how it was. Fus had invalidated everything, and even though Gillou could have got into the very best schools, it was all over. Jérémy was stuck in the same dilemma. I said to Jérémy: "You could still make it. Abandon us, nobody will mind. Leave us, you won't get anything out of it. You're like my son, you are my son, but he's not your brother, he's just a guy you knew when you were younger, and you'd lost sight of for years, so don't let yourself rot for the rest of your life, move away from him, he's toxic." I said all that to Jérémy but he stayed. He smiled at me, a bit stupidly, the smile of someone already contaminated, who had already accepted that there would be nothing else to do. Nothing was ever going to rival what had been done. The damage was huge for Gillou. To start with, at the end of the year he would pay for his sleepless nights and the classes he had skipped for all those prison visits whose dates kept changing, timetables that made no sense, scheduled for the middle of the week and then cancelled at the last minute. It wasn't just his end-of-year exams! I don't know how Gillou viewed his life now, this brother who he would have to visit regularly and who would never leave him be. At what point, when you met a girl, did you confess that your brother was in jail for years and years? What would you tell her when she wanted to know why? That was what awaited Gillou, a shitty life that would rotate forever on a single axis, the penitentiary center of his brother. And if he tried to forget, to go far away, abroad, perhaps, so as not to be on prison duty every month, a terrible remorse would seize him by the throat and never let go. I almost got off more easily in a sense. I had less of my life to live, and I'd accepted things. I'd agreed to be an unworthy father who wouldn't set foot in prison and I didn't care about the disapproval of Jacky or *la moman* up there.

When the police came knocking at my door a few weeks later, I was watching TV, and at the sight of the rotating police lights illuminating the whole district and bouncing off the walls, I immediately thought something must have happened at the prison. That Fus had taken a beating. And that this time he hadn't made it out alive. For a second I didn't know if I was relieved or not. But that wasn't why they had come. They'd come to tell me that the investigation was being reopened. I went and collapsed on the sofa. The Tour de France was on television. A breakaway, maybe one that was going to get to the finishing line. I could hear the joy in the commentators' voices, I could hear that world going on living. My son was still alive and suddenly, although I didn't know why, I felt happy again. It was a happiness that I hadn't known in years. A happiness that stayed with me all evening. I went and sat in his room, I breathed in the smell of his blankets and fell asleep thinking about him, praying that he would sleep well, that he too, like me, would hear the sound of the night. This time Fus's face as a child mingled with Fus's face as a prisoner. It was my son who was sleeping on that horrible bed, taking advantage of a few hours of respite before the prison noises started up again. It was my son being gently reconciled.

THE NEXT DAY I went to the stadium. Before the guys got there. I sat down in my seat. The pitch had suffered in the heat. It was the very end of the season, maybe the last training session before the break, I wasn't exactly sure. The players arrived one by one. More or less awake, more or less fresh. But apart from two or three newcomers who I didn't know, one by one they had come to say hello, clenched fist, hand on heart, as if it was something they did all the time. Without a word. Mechanically. No need to say a thing. It was better that way. I knew who I was, where we had ended up. Only one of them asked after Fus, and was he bearing up. "I think so," I said. "Yeah. He'll be fine," he replied before moving off into the middle of the pitch. The session had gone well, it already felt restful, the guys went easy, no injuries before the holidays. I let them leave again. Then I picked up a bit of the grass, where it was still more or less healthy-looking. I filled up a little Tupperware tub with it and then called Fus's lawyer. He was happy with the way things were turning out and the new evidence that he'd collected — I think he was happy that I was a bit more motivated — and advised me to approach Fus's girlfriend so that we could coordinate. I didn't understand his interest, but he insisted: "It's better, believe me, it'll be better if everyone sings from the same hymn sheet." When I got to Krystyna's house I was no longer sure of myself. Her father opened the door. He had come to the trial on the day when his daughter was giving testimony. I didn't know what he thought about all that, if he wished we would go to hell, me and my son. Agitating for Le Pen was one thing, quite another to see his daughter caught up with a guy who was going to spend half his life in jail. He was surprised, but he ushered me in. His detached house was pretty much like ours, maybe a bit smaller. The same furniture. The same things on the wall. Family photographs on the sideboard. They showed Krystyna accompanied in all her childhood photographs by a bigger girl — her sister? — who disappeared from the more recent ones. Her father offered me a seat at the dining-room table – their little sitting room was full of baskets of ironing and clothes hung over the backs of the two armchairs. "I do the ironing in this house. Forgive the mess." I couldn't stop looking at the photographs of Krystyna. A girl without a story. Not very expressive. Not particularly pretty. Far from ugly too. Once he'd gone to get me something to drink, and left me with plenty of time to study everything there was to study in his dining room, he started sighing. Not in a mean way, just annoyed that he had nothing to say to me. Or else he didn't know where to start. At last he launched off: "Krystyna's mother left last year. Don't ask me where. Probably to follow our older daughter, but I'm not sure. We've had no news from either of them." He went on to tell me about their lives: the sister had left three years ago, they'd never really got on very well. All the politics hadn't helped, but to be honest that wasn't what they'd fought over. It was the same thing with the mother. Of course, she'd been cross with him and Krystyna for getting mixed up with that guy – "well, I mean, with your son," he apologized – but if she left it was just because things weren't going very well. "I'm worried sick about Krystyna," he said to me. "I've stopped sleeping. I don't know where it's all going to take us. She loves your son. But we can agree, can't we, that it isn't a solution? My daughter's still young." I agreed with him. I couldn't wish for anyone to waste their life like that. To wait for the release of a kid who would be ruined by years of prison, who would have no job, no situation when he left. Probably medicated up to the eyeballs. Wrecked by the violence in jail. I couldn't wish for anyone to have to take endless trips to go and see him – now he was still in Metz-Queuleu, but where would he be tomorrow? – to have to write to him, to have to think about him, maybe to have to be faithful to him. Such a calling had to be reserved only for those who couldn't act otherwise. For those who had no other choice. The strictest intimacy. I included Gillou in that, unfortunately for him. I included Jérémy, because I knew he could survive it. I included Jacky, because he was a stubborn as a mule and he would know how to go on living. I included myself in it too, now. But I agreed with Krystyna's father, that poor girl had nothing to do with the whole thing. I said that to her father. It seemed to reassure him, I also told him I had no idea how to get there. He would know better than I did how to persuade his daughter. He looked at me for a long time, completely disarmed. He poured me another drink. He started sighing again, looking at his hands. Damn it all, where was the militant fascist who was so sure of his cause? I could see only a pitiful figure, like me, and equally confused. "They've messed us up something rotten, haven't they, with their nonsense," he said. And that "nonsense" on his lips – I don't think I'm wrong in saying this – wasn't our children's nonsense, it wasn't that, it was something higher, something more ungraspable, which went beyond us and out into the great expanses. In the end, it was our own nonsense, everything that we had done and perhaps, first and foremost, everything we hadn't done. The lawyer didn't agree with our way of looking at things, he needed Krystyna, he needed her to be motivated. Or at least as convincing as she was at the first trial.

The lawyer was flailing. So was I, by now. I'd finally understood that Fus's life had been overturned over a mere nothing. That all of our lives, in spite of their incredible surface linearity, were mere accidents, random events, missed meetings and encounters. Our lives were filled with that great multitude of nothings which, depending how we managed them, would make us either kings of the world or jailbirds. "I was there at the right time" – that was what people who had made it could confess. I was there at the right time when I met *la moman*. If she'd arrived a few minutes later at the youth club we wouldn't have met. We weren't from the same parts, there was no reason why we'd ever have seen each other. We would have set off on two trajectories, the nothings would have multiplied, we would have had other children, it would have been different. Fus had been there at the wrong time. When he had bumped into the gang. The rest had been sparked by that. At the bad moment when he went back to attack the guy. If we put the concatenation of facts together, there were thousands of cases in which that day didn't end as cruelly. If we wanted to be fair, perhaps hundreds that would still end with the death of that kid. But I didn't plan to say that at the trial. The kid was called Julien. It had taken me some time to give him a first name. When you were called Julien, you'd enjoyed a reasonable amount of love from your parents, you hadn't known poverty or war, how did you end up in a gang, by what sudden boost of violence – when you're called Julien – did you end up on the ground, your skull smashed, in the gutter? It was part of the great mystery of nothings. I wrote to his parents. I didn't know if I was allowed to. I told them there wasn't a day when I didn't think about our two sons. I even told them I'd rather it had been mine who had died, that for me it was the same thing; it was obviously incredibly clumsy and stupid to say that, and if I'd thought about it, it was no longer true. But I think they understood the idea, because they replied. They'd started their letter by saying they were shocked that there might be an appeal. They didn't want to start all over again, they didn't have the will. But no sooner had they said that than they assured me that they understood that we might want to defend ourselves. They prayed a lot, it did them good, I should try it. In their letter they never referred to Fus. They talked to me. They forgave me. They concluded with an odd phrase about the pointlessness of prison. I didn't know if they were going to mention that again at the trial.

That minute when everything went off the rails might equally never have happened, never have existed. It didn't detract from Fus's basic responsibility, but it made him less alone, less monstrous. Those were the foundations on which I did my work. Through acquaintances I had found some members of the gang. They weren't choirboys. The first contact had been rough. Luckily I had Jacky and two other tough guys from the section with me. We immediately had to tell the guys that we weren't there to stir shit, but that something that should have stayed a fistfight between two groups had degenerated into something else. They told me their mate Julien had been attacked from behind by a fascist with an iron bar. That they didn't see the fistfight I described, it was anything but a fistfight, there were rules about fistfights, they were pretty well known, and even when they clashed with other gangs, even when things got really wild, they punched guys in the face and didn't whack them from behind. In this case nothing had been respected. And the fact that the fascist was my son made no difference to anything. I didn't reply. There wasn't much to say in reply, and I didn't hope for anything from that first meeting. I came back with a photograph of Fus when he came out of hospital, which we'd had to take for the insurance. You could clearly see the huge hole behind his ear. "There you go, guys, that's you," I said. "A hole in the head, four days in, but in a coma, neurological aftereffects. I don't bear a grudge against any of you, you got caught up in the heat of the moment. I didn't bring you any pictures of the girl, but I don't imagine there's much point, and I guess you remember pretty clearly what state you left her in." They looked at me. They swapped glances to see who was going to react. I went on: "At that moment, when you decided to attack them, the only mistake that girl and my son the fascist had made was handing out pamphlets by Le Pen. I agree with you that you don't have to be particularly clever to do that, that you have to be particularly stupid, and even passably much of a bastard to dish out that shit, but there you are, apart from all that, they hadn't asked anything of you. They didn't ask you to come into their lives that day, they didn't ask you to beat the hell out of them as you did. So whether you hit them from the front, from behind, with simple knuckledusters or nunchucks, it wouldn't have made much difference, the result would have been pretty much the same." "What do you want us to say?" the oldest member of the gang asked me. "You don't have to say anything to me," I replied, "I just want you to explain how that happens, let's say, if you want, how that should happen, I want you to tell the court that it went particularly stupid this time. I want you to acknowledge that my son might have had one or two reasons to come and take his revenge, I want you to say that maybe he just wanted to whack Julien in the face, that he didn't necessarily mean it to end like that . . ." "But your son only messed up one of his blows," he cut in. "Don't you worry about that, just explain how you conduct your fights, and it will be up to his lawyer to get people to understand that sometimes, once you've got going, once you're blinded by rage and fear, you can't stop in time." Getting them to make statements wasn't easy. Two of them pulled out, we managed to get a sworn recording out of a third, in which he told the story of the fight, masked and with his voice disguised. In it he put a lot of the blame on his mates, Julien included.

The appeal procedure was shorter, more in Fus's favor. Julien's parents only came on one day, having said that they'd already given their statements and they didn't think there was any need to give Fus a harsher sentence, the lad had already been punished enough. More importantly, they explained that their son had some responsibility in the case. That echoed the testimony of Julien's mate and, for the first time, we had a better sense of why one fine morning Fus wanted to go out for a fight. The others, the football trainer and Jacky, did their bit. I was also a bit more convincing. I told them about the zombie that Fus had been when he came out of hospital. How I'd had to help him with everything. For the first few days he couldn't even eat without making a mess. For the first few nights he had pissed himself. That's what I said, things I didn't want to say the first time. The lawyer didn't need to torture me, it all came naturally: how we'd had go back to the ER when he fainted in the toilet, how for days he hadn't managed to utter a single word. How he'd been sluggish, feeble almost, when his brother had come back on Saturday. At the end I summed up my mistakes, everything the lawyer had made me say at the first trial. I didn't say anything about the bar, that famous iron bar, which Fus must have worked on so that it would do even more damage. I recognized that bar, a bar I'd brought back from the workshop, which I'd used as a winch, it was round at the time, not sharp and jagged as it was now, in its plastic bag. I kept my trap shut at the first trial and I hadn't opened it again at the second, the damage was done. In any case, no one denied that Fus had used a weapon, and whether it was round or pointed, what difference could it make? The lawyer said the bar had been brought along just in case, that Fus didn't know how many people he might come across. When he'd left the house the bar was there for self-defense, not to kill. Why not. Doubt. Introduce doubt.

When you put all those things together it came to twelve years. I had a dizzy spell when I heard the sentence, deeply disappointed that it was still so severe, as if I'd forgotten that my son had killed someone. Twelve years was still an enormously long time. The lawyer was satisfied. The sentence had been reduced by half. If Fus kept his nose clean, he could negotiate a remission. In the end he might be inside for eight or nine years. He'd already spent over a year behind bars. I left him to his calculations. Jacky got me plastered that evening. We went and sat in a bar in Nancy and got straight on the whisky. At first he held back, with a view to driving me back to the village. But in the end we had to call his wife to come and get us. We'd made her do a two-hour trip in the middle of the night, but that didn't seem so serious, she seemed to understand, and seemed almost reassured that it was only that. In the car, when we'd recovered our senses a bit, he confessed that he didn't know what to think. He was more detached from everything, he had a clearer view of what happened, he had been immersed in both trials, and perhaps he was better able to anticipate the jury's clemency? That didn't stop him weeping in my arms the next day and the day after that. "At least we're mates again," he said.

THE PRISON VISITS always made my head spin. However much I tried, I couldn't get used to it. I had nightmares several days before, but sure, once I was in there it was pretty much OK, I didn't have the crazy desire to escape as soon as I got there like I had at the beginning. I managed to look at my Fus a little, check that he'd shaved, that he was taking care of himself a bit. He was wearing clothes that I'd brought him the last time, I think he looked after them, I think he knew how revolted I was by everything and didn't want to add to it. So when I saw that he was clean that was pretty much OK, I forgot that he was a prisoner, I managed to blur out the rest a bit. I liked going there with Jacky, because he wasn't apprehensive about it, he just made himself comfortable in there as if he was in a bar, he was at ease with everyone, he hadn't an ounce of shame. Jacky preferred that we went in one at a time, "that means more visits for the kid." So I resigned myself to going in alone. The first months had been awkward, for me, also for Fus. I felt he was absent. I didn't know if it was the aftereffects of the illness or if he was being stuffed full of medication. I asked Gillou if he'd noticed the same thing but he wasn't paying attention. When he went there he spoke, he put on a show, he wouldn't let Fus get a word in. There was a point to it. With all the stories, summaries of soaps, streams of sketches that he told him, Fus had enough to keep him going for a week. "But when you tell him all your nonsense does that make him laugh?" I asked him. He said uncertainly, "Yeah, yeah. Pretty much, don't worry about it."

Then things seemed to have sorted themselves out. They changed his cell. Fus started talking again. Asking after people. And telling me about himself. His days, his evenings. The gym. The little library. "I can bring you some books if you want." "Yes, if you want." That kind of conversation. It wasn't huge but we were coming back together after a long time apart. We easily filled our hour. Of course there were silences, but they were useful, it wasn't wasted visiting time. We took advantage of them to look at each other a bit, smile at each other again. Tame each other. When I got home in the evening I did some calculations, I looked at the internet, I called the lawyer the next day. How much time did he have left? I wanted him to be nice to the prison guards, to keep his nose clean, I waited for partial amnesties, I read up on prison overpopulation, I reflected that things might be going his way, that we'd get him out, I called Jacky and asked him what he thought, and I wrote to the lawyer again. I started going mad. I relived the final illness of *la moman*, whole days spent waiting for something a little bit better, the ill-considered hopes in any bit of news, and I experienced again the fear and revulsion of hospital, the great weariness of those visits, and here everything was amplified a hundred, a thousand times. So it was a relief, a consolation to see that Fus was talking again, that he was a bit interested in the world. We didn't address everything directly. He had paid a high enough price for confrontations. So we commented instead, we were careful about what we said. We took more account, sat there on our stools, of the weight and violence of opinions. We swapped articles. I kept cuttings of football stories for him, news about FC Metz, articles from *Le Répub* for subscribers only. I also kept pieces about anything concerning the future of the region. He liked it when I told him someone was building a small factory, it didn't happen all that often. He followed in detail the studies and progress of Gillou and Jérémy, and he explained to me the subtleties, all the possibilities that were opening up to them. That little routine allowed me to handle the situation better, and maybe in five years' time I'd get there.

Deep down, I knew we were condemned to this halfway house as long as we didn't talk about what happened. I wanted to know if he had any remorse, if it stopped him from sleeping as it did me. But he never talked about it. On the contrary, I had a sense that he was going through everything mechanically, with incredible detachment. He talked to me without horror, clinically, about what his fellow inmates had done. As if it was a simple game of debits and credits. As if the sentences they were serving were quite enough to repay their debts. And in that he was no different from the rest.

Krystyna didn't come back to see him after the trial. I had a long discussion with her. I didn't feel that she was in love with my son – she'd more or less confirmed as much – so I didn't understand what made her stay in touch with him. She was like a loyal sister who was forcing herself to fulfill some sort of vow. I wanted to make sure at all costs that she didn't lock herself up in that, that she didn't turn it into a horrible habit. I told her she wouldn't stay the course, I described to her what twelve years of imprisonment really was, how many visits that meant. She understood. Most of all she understood that it would hurt him much more if she left him in a year or two than if she left him now. I thanked her for what she had said at the trial, but she'd done enough. Then she admitted to me that she'd had an abortion a week after Fus had killed Julien. That it wasn't a small thing, that Fus had never known he was a father. The day she had come to our house, the day she had come to fire him up with her stories of revenge, she could have told him about that tiny thing. That tiny thing that was nothing at all. Already gone today.

Dear Dad,

By the time you read these words, I will already be on my way. You need rest, there's no point in your exhausting yourself like this on these pointless trips. It's high time I let you go. Gillou will soon be a father – it's a little boy, I hope I'm not the first to break it to you! – and his wife doesn't like knowing he's here. I can see that. He has better things to do with his time. You too will soon have better things to do, with the little one! Teach him to ride a bike, go slowly at the beginning, there's no point making him take the calvary slope like you did with Gillou and me. Take your time with him, take him to the stadium, take him to the cemetery if you want. Kids like playing among the graves. Of course there's only three years to wait, three years is nothing given how long I've waited already, but I'm sure they'll be your three best years. I don't want to take them away from you. Yesterday I learned that they planned to transfer me soon, yet again! It would only have been a longer journey for you both, and I can't inflict that on you, so I've decided to get away. This distance will do us good. Even Krystyna who had forgotten me has started writing again! Thank Jérémy and Jacky for all they've done for me, I haven't the time or the courage to write to them, but I think about them a lot. Say goodbye to la moman *for me. Give my brother a big hug. I don't regret anything about my life, at any rate not the one we lived together. I think it was a beautiful life. Others will say it was a shitty life, a life of pain and tragedy, but I say it was a beautiful life.*

A hug from me,
Fus

Notes

1 Louis Aragon, 1897–1972, Surrealist poet, novelist and Communist. Gustave Eiffel, 1832–1923, engineer noted for building railway bridges and the Eiffel Tower. Guy Môquet, 1924–1941, a Communist activist executed by the Nazis when he was only seventeen.

2 Jean Ferrat, 1930–2010, French singer best known for his settings of Louis Aragon. This song is about Robert Desnos, 1900–1945, Surrealist poet, who died in Theresienstadt concentration camp.

3 CGT: Confédération Générale du Travail, or General Confederation of Labour, powerful French trade union.

4 Groupe Union Défense, the far-right students' union.

LAURENT PETITMANGIN was born in 1965 in the east of France into a family of railway workers. He has received numerous literary prizes in France for his writing, including the Prix Femina des lycéens, the Prix Stanislas, the Grand Prix du premier roman, as well as numerous readers' prizes. *What You Need from the Night* is his debut novel.

SHAUN WHITESIDE has translated numerous books from German, French, Italian, and Dutch, including novels by Amélie Nothomb, Luther Blissett, Wu Ming, and Marcel Möring, as well as eight in Georges Simenon's Maigret series. His most recent translations from French include *Serotonin* by Michel Houellebecq and *Deer Man* by Geoffroy Delorme. He lives in London.